The One That I Want

Michelle Monkou

D0012389

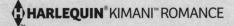

H HARLEQUIN® KIMANI™ ROMANCE

Recycling programs
for this product may
not exist in your area.

ISBN-13: 978-0-373-86516-1

The One That I Want

Copyright © 2017 by Michelle Monkou

Printed in U.S.A.

www.Harlequin.com

Michelle Monkou became a world traveler at the age of three, when she left her birthplace of London, England, and moved to Guyana, South America. She then moved to the US as a young teen. Michelle was nominated for the 2003 Emma Award for Favorite New Author, and continues to write romances with complex characters and intricate plots.

Visit her website for further information at www.michellemonkou.com or contact her at michellemonkou@comcast.net.

Books by Michelle Monkou

Harlequin Kimani Romance

Sweet Surrender
Here and Now
Straight to the Heart
No One But You
Gamble on Love
Only in Paradise
Trail of Kisses
The Millionaire's Ultimate Catch
If I Had You
Racing Hearts
Passionate Game
One of a Kind
One to Love
One to Win
The One That I Want

Visit the Author Profile page at Harlequin.com for more titles.

To the Harlequin Kimani staff, thank you for the many years of support to bring my stories to life.

Acknowledgments

With the recent passing of my mother, it has been a time of loss and reflection. I want to extend my appreciation and gratitude for the kind words and thoughts during this time from Glenda Howard, Shannon Criss, Carly Silver and Keyla Hernandez. Your continued support helped with the completion of this book and series.

"You're the perfect superhero type," she mused.

"Now you're being cruel."

"Nope. It's always the quiet types who have the deepest strength. The others are brute force and brawn. Boring. The intellectuals have a delightful way of taking their time, stroking their way, biding their time to the happy ending."

He puffed up his chest. "Yeah. Do I need an *S* on my chest?"

"No, you need something original. Mysterious, dark, brooding."

"I don't brood."

"You think hard." She smiled. "Better."

"Every superhero needs a leading lady."

"Are you holding auditions?"

"Only have one person in mind."

"I wonder who that will be."

"She'll know. They always know that they are the one."

"But then they let the superhero go because he's got a destiny bigger than hers."

"Or she takes a step back out of fear."

Laxmi stopped eating and pointed her chopsticks at him. "What woman has been afraid to step up to be with her superhero?"

Dear Reader,

In this latest installment, the Meadows family have all had their adventures. I hope that you've stayed with each cousin to enjoy her unique journey to self-discovery and love. Coming from a small family, I always imagined what a large extended one would be like—maybe a little comedy, a lot of drama, but love and loyalty would always rule.

With each story, I wanted to bring challenges and opportunities that were relatable and entertaining. Our heartstrings needed a little tugging as we witnessed the romance and all it meant as each couple's life blossomed in a special way.

I hope that, in your life, you are surrounded by a circle of friends, family and relatives who are bringing joy, laughter and much love to your space.

May your dreams come true,

Michelle

Chapter 1

Dresden Haynes stepped in from the biting, wintry mix into the cozy warmth of his parents' home. Instead of the customary deluge of holiday decorations to usher in Christmas, the first floor was an exhibition of widespread chaos. For the first time in a while, he wouldn't spend the holidays with his parents. This time he'd stay in Toronto while his parents, Patrick and Charlotte, no-longer-retired globe-trekkers, soon would be off to Kazakhstan as engineering consultants for a three-year stint on a water treatment contract.

This latest nudge to rock his routine off-kilter was one of many this year. All of it, especially a surprise meet-up with some members of his birth family and now the lengthy absence of his adoptive family, was out of his comfort zone.

Frenzied sounds of his parents' preparations hit him in intermittent bursts. Overhead his father's frustrations verbally punctuated the air just before loud, dull thuds and dragging sounds scraped against the ceiling. An assortment of suitcases blocked access to the staircase. Meanwhile, brown boxes outlined a path toward the kitchen, where he saw his mother with her sleeves rolled up.

Taking careful steps, he navigated his way through the foyer, around the assortment of boxes and down the hallway. Her determined expression remained rigid as she looked up at an awful abstract painting above the pantry door. He bit back the smile over her loud, dramatic sighs that floated toward him.

"Bought it at a yard sale. I think you should take it." Charlotte shifted her attention as he approached to greet her with a kiss on the cheek.

"Let the new renters enjoy it." Dresden failed to hide his shudder at the hideous collision of colors that masqueraded as art.

"You could move in until we return."

"Nope. I like my place just fine." His parents had chosen the suburbs, but he liked downtown Toronto with its beehive busyness. "And you know that my commute is closer to the university."

"At least keep an eye on the place while we're gone."

"Stop worrying. I'll play the grumpy landlord whenever necessary." Dresden playfully bumped his mother's shoulder. "Dutiful son. History professor. Landlord—I'm your best son ever." And she was the best mother ever.

"Don't run off our renters, either." His mother softly slapped his arm.

Dresden nodded, also hoping she wouldn't add last-minute items to his list of tasks.

Charlotte bustled past him toward the stove and lifted the lid off a small pot. "I don't have much in the house to make a meal. Your dad and I've been eating out for the past two days. That's tiresome and not great food. This morning's feast?" She scrunched her nose to mimic his reaction to the offering of congealed oatmeal.

Dresden shook his head. "I'm fine. Ate not too long ago."

"What brings you here? Not that I'm unhappy to see you. But we did have a really nice goodbye dinner with you last night," she said as she opened cabinets, inspected the empty space and pulled out any forgotten items.

What did bring him there? A need. One that gnawed at his center. Although he suffered no physical pain, he felt a heaviness as the day broke and the hours until his parents' departure grew closer.

"Thought you might need a hand. No matter how much you plan, there is always something that goes off-script. Decided to pop over, just in case..." He shrugged out of his jacket, tossed it on a chair and joined her with inspecting the higher out-of-reach cabinets.

"We're fine. Movers will be here within the hour. And I do have one more day before boarding the plane." She paused and a hint of a frown flittered on her forehead. "You, however, don't have one more day to face your destiny."

Dresden stared into the empty space of a cabinet. Not a speck of dirt in sight. However, his mood mirrored the bleak emptiness of the shelves. The void in his soul couldn't give a glimpse of the future, and it didn't offer any solutions, either.

The blame for his unsettled feelings sat squarely at one person—Verona, his birth mother—and her family, the Meadowses.

His parents, whom he refused to think of in any other capacity, had never hid the fact that he was adopted. They'd never shared the details, allowing him to choose whether he wanted to know. And he didn't. Had no desire to unseat his parents from their position in his life.

But when Grace Meadows took his choice away with her revealing letter, the surprise had sucked the breath out of his lungs. She'd forced him to face the truth, to acknowledge that another woman and her family were connected to him. Her entreaty, though polite, had shredded his world, leaving him to question how he should or should not feel.

Then, like an encore performance, Leo Starks, her lawyer, further made inroads with his heartbreaking story about the loss of his family and finding love again with Fiona, Grace's granddaughter. That same granddaughter, his half sister, had managed to breach his defensive wall with her fresh outlook and honesty, to extend a hand of friendship. One that he'd accepted, but not without conditions. He wanted nothing to do with Verona—the woman who'd given birth to him.

Despite his rules of engagement, because he was a Meadows, with their international news and lifestyle media empire, the media spotlight had turned on him. Why did the Meadowses have the power to whip up a fog of confusion around his life?

Dresden sighed, wishing for more palatable options to materialize for his sake.

"You've got to attend Grace Meadows's birthday party." Charlotte had a knack for delivering the toughest messages wrapped in soothing tones and gentle smiles. "You've already booked your flight for tonight. No procrastinating."

"I can meet them anytime."

"It's your grandmother's eightieth birthday."

"Grace." He couldn't help the correction. Only in his thoughts did he play with such familiar terms of his birth family. Grandmother. Mother. Sister. But to say those words aloud and attach them to the respective member of the Meadows family—well, he couldn't stop the constriction that gripped his throat when he envisioned the scenario.

"Go celebrate Grace's life. She would love seeing you there."

"How would you know?" He turned his back and busied himself with inspecting another set of cabinets.

"Because I want them to see what a wonderful and respectable man you've turned out to be."

Throughout his childhood, to him, his mother was the average working mom. To his school friends, she had this larger-than-life persona, like a female Indiana Jones, who wasn't afraid to work in faraway, sometimes dangerous, places.

"Ah...so that's the true reason you want me to go. For your glory," he teased.

"Can you blame me? We'd hoped you'd be prepared for this eventuality. That's why we never hid your adoption from you. Nothing to be ashamed or afraid of by you or by us. Besides, you're a dashing gentleman. With a forgiving heart...right?"

Dresden's laughter erupted into a roar that took a few seconds to die down. "You certainly know how to flatter and sway the wind to your favor."

"That's how I got your dad." Charlotte retrieved his jacket, handing it to him. Then she slipped her hand through his arm. "Now, come with me." She tightened her grip and walked him out of the kitchen and down the hallway. "You shouldn't waste another minute trying to figure out your next step. You already know."

"I'm feeling manhandled," he protested.

"And you'd be absolutely right." They made it into the foyer. Her hand still wound around his arm.

"Is that you, Dresden? I'm coming right down." His father's footsteps crossed the room overhead.

"No need to come down, Patrick," his mother shouted up the stairs. "He's heading out now." She opened the door and, with more muscle than Dresden was prepared for, pushed him outside onto the porch.

"Really, you want me to go hobnob with the Meadowses." All kidding aside, Dresden couldn't believe how adamant his mother was on the issue.

"Yep, pretty much. I want you to be kind and make that old woman happy."

"I agree with your mother. Go and show respect for your elders." His father popped into view next to his wife.

They were the trifecta of a perfect match, with brains, beauty and marital bliss. Way beyond his talent and abilities. His parents were a unique couple who enjoyed their intense, but sometimes chaotic, lives. To Dresden, they had set the bar on life and love way too high for him to successfully follow.

"Don't think she'd want to be called old," Dresden muttered. Suffering under the wintry conditions, his teeth chattered, joining in with the uncontrollable shivering of his body.

"Good. Later you can share with me what other things she doesn't like."

"I didn't say that I'd go."

"They aren't the bad guys in your story. Right now, it might feel that way. But, trust me, after a few more decades of life under your belt, you may feel differently."

"Well, until that time comes—"

His mother interrupted with her palm raised in the universal stop sign. "We'll see you in the spring. Skype and FaceTime will be our means for chatting. I do love you, son. But you've got a birthday party to run off to. Stop dawdling."

The door closed. Lock turned.

Dresden blew on his frozen fingers, hoping she was kidding. Not until his ears started to suffer from stinging numbness did he declare defeat. Dresden flipped up the collar of his jacket to ward off the frigid temperature. He headed toward his car to retreat from the battle.

Laxmi Holder's party days were long over. Now she was staying out of the spotlight, in case any lingering fans recognized her; that had prompted her low profile, especially on social media. Now she was the average citizen, trying to get her daily hustle on from her home base of Brooklyn instead of Los Angeles. From being a singer to managing one, she had switched viewpoints on the same playground.

Returning home meant that she could either reestablish her friendships or make new ones. Her retention rate on that front was abysmal, except for one friend—Fiona Meadows—with whom she really wanted to invest the time to rebuild their bond.

She reread the invitation that Fiona had hand-delivered to her. The Meadowses were celebrating the matriarch's—Grace's—birthday. It took a bit of cajoling from Fiona to get her to respond in the affirmative.

The excitement over going to the media mogul's birthday gave way to a case of dread a few hours before she was due to leave for the party. She wasn't a celebrity—got close, though. Then her career had suffered a fastburn to nothing.

A wardrobe of nice clothes, a fast sports car and tiny savings were the remnants of her former life. Now she'd have to go among New York's elite and the world's richest and pretend that she belonged.

"Well, here goes nothing," she remarked to her mirrored reflection before heading out.

* * *

Five hours later Dresden exited New York City's John F. Kennedy Airport and stepped into the waiting limo. Unless he grabbed the driver by the shoulder in a fit of panic to force a detour, Dresden was bound for the iconic Winthorpe International Hotel.

The saying "sit back and enjoy the ride" didn't really hold true. He was far from comfortable in the quiet, luxurious confines of the limo. Standing in front of a college class of forty to fifty university students talking about Canada's natives, settlers and conquistadors didn't faze him. But heading to a birthday party in one of the swankiest New York City hotels, with New York's elite, for one of New York's most influential moguls—who happened to be his grandmother—turned his gut into a queasy mess.

Dresden kept up a steady routine of rubbing his hands along his pant legs as the limo sped along to its destination. The clammy state of his palms didn't bode well. People would shake his hand and give him the side-eye of disgust.

Horns blared. Messengers on bikes shouted warnings. Tour buses rumbled along with camera-ready riders. The New York City vibe had an effective way of delivering a potent shot of adrenaline to the system. With nervous energy already pumping through him, his pulse stayed at hyper level. He offered up a prayer of gratitude as the limo pulled up in front of the hotel. He needed his feet on firm ground.

A grinning uniformed porter briefly touched the brim of his cap before holding open the limo door. "Welcome to the Winthorpe. It's our pleasure to be of service."

"Thank you." Dresden shoved his hands deep into his coat pockets, now feeling more than a bit self-conscious about its average, off-the-rack style. Even the staff out-styled him with their crisp white gloves.

"Any luggage?" The porter looked questioningly at the driver then at Dresden.

"None. I'm here for the Meadows reception."

"Please step inside with your invitation and you'll be escorted to the event."

Dresden retrieved the important gold-embossed pass-port from his pocket and complied with the porter's instructions.

In the lobby a dedicated attendant for the reception checked the invitation and escorted him to the ballroom's entrance. There, a second attendant checked his invitation against a computerized list. Like a baton handed over for the next leg of the trip, a third attendant escorted him into the ballroom.

The expansive size of the room, the over one hundred decorated tables and chairs, the high ratio of staff to guests—all conspired to push his pulse into overdrive. He almost bumped into a passing waiter as he gaped at every drip and drop of glitz and glamour. Lifestyles of the rich and famous gathered under one roof.

As they were about to head down the middle of the room to what he presumed to be the head table, Dresden needed a minute to get the nerves under control. His heart raced as if amped by a massive dose of adrenaline. Although not hit by dizziness, he couldn't ignore the out-of-body sensation that occurred with each step. He wasn't in control. This wasn't on his turf. The realization pressed in on his chest, impeding airflow. He tried not to pant like an out-of-shape jogger.

His escort looked back at the door, probably wishing someone more interesting and actually famous had been his assignment.

"I'm good. Gonna get a drink first." Dresden pointed to the nearest bar. "I'll find my way to the principal's office." He laughed. The attendant didn't.

No longer under anyone's responsibility, Dresden followed through on his word and headed for a bar a few feet away. Too bad the bar didn't come equipped with stools. He'd gladly grab one and nurse a beer for the duration. No one would ever have to know that he was there. But for actual records, the check-in list would show that he'd arrived. Immediately his mother's caution piled onto his guilt. The Meadowses weren't owed his compliance.

Laxmi would have returned home if Fiona hadn't spotted her in the room. She felt nauseous by the time she'd gone through the checkpoints to get into the party. At any moment, she expected someone to accuse her of being a faker.

"I'm so glad you made it." Fiona hugged her tight, making Laxmi gasp. "Thought you would bail on me."

"Of course not. Wouldn't dream of it." Laxmi hid her lie behind a bright grin. "Feels like most of New York is in this room."

"It's a good turnout." Fiona looked radiant. Her fierce detective persona had disappeared behind stylish hair and makeup. She looked gorgeous in her evening dress.

Maybe she shouldn't have worn the minidress. But she needed the safety net of her former style as the brash, youthful party girl. She could observe the world through that veneer.

"Come. Come. Let me show you to the head table."

"Oh, no. I could have had a seat in the back. Near the coat check."

"You're so silly." Fiona laughed, but as if sensing the

retreat, she hooked her arm through Laxmi's and guided her to the table.

After introductions were made, Laxmi took her seat.

Fiona patted her shoulder. "Sorry, I'm going to have to leave you. Have to play hostess."

"Oh, please, go do your thing. I'll be fine." Laxmi waved her on and tried to keep her nerves away from her smile.

But once Fiona left, she felt alone. Stranded. No one at the table talked to her. The cousins might have remembered her, but she had been close to only Fiona. With the event not ready to start officially for thirty minutes, she scanned the room for a place to hang. The minibars stationed around the big room seemed good enough. She made her escape.

"Is this spot taken?"

Dresden shook his head without bothering to look over his shoulder. He wasn't interested in conversation, even if its owner's fragrance smelled so damn good it baited his curiosity to check her out. To distract himself, he shifted his focus to the head table and scanned the faces, looking for one specifically—Fiona, the only tolerable Meadow and his half sister.

"Which Meadows do you know?"

Dresden blinked and reluctantly turned to the woman who prodded his attention and who couldn't read a vibe. Irritation fueled his impatience with the invader. His self-exile was on the verge of a breach.

A smile, bold and bright, greeted him and sucked the wind from his lungs. Its owner held out her hand to match the cheeriness behind her flash of teeth. "Laxmi Holder."

The second after she said her name he silently repeated *Lak-shmee*.

He shook her hand and didn't want to let go. But he had to when her smile turned into a bubbly burst of laughter at his flustered reaction. His face flushed with the creeping heat from his neck up over his cheeks.

An awkward handshake was the least of his problems as his eyes connected with her face.

Sexy, full lips were splashed with a badass red color. Bright eyes popped because of long, dark lashes and shapely arched brows. Add the interesting contours of her face and he might as well have stepped off the edge and fallen into a delightful rabbit hole.

"And you are?" she prompted. She hadn't broken eye contact now that he couldn't stop staring at her.

"Dresden." He sipped his drink to quell the sudden dryness.

"You're one of those one-name celebrities—like Cher and Madonna?"

He laughed at the idea of being anything but a history professor working on his genealogy as a personal hobby. Still, he jumped on the option to keep his last name out of the mix since he had no idea in what social circle she spent her time. His new fame had brought him into the spotlight with the details trickling in or being sensationalized for the gossip spreads. Any public mention of his life stripped away his privacy that he'd taken for granted. Reading the fictional and even the nonfictional bits about his life sounded insignificant and average when splashed against the Meadowses' powerful reputation.

"Okay, mystery man," she said in a husky voice that sounded like an old jazz singer's. "We'll play it your way. I like solving puzzles."

"Nothing much to know." And he meant it as a curtain to keep out her curiosity.

She shrugged, but he saw the interest intensify like

so many did at mention of the Meadowses. She looked poised for any discovery. Her gaze recorded everything. If he stumbled and opened access to his life, she'd pounce without hesitation. While he had no intention of opening up about who he was because who really knew what had triggered her attention? On the other hand, he didn't want his reluctance to end their conversation.

"Mild temperatures for the time of the year. More than chilly tonight, though."

Laxmi signaled to the bartender for a refill. "Looks like we'll stay in the safe zone and chat about the weather. Or maybe we can talk politics?"

Dresden made a face. "That's depressing."

She tapped her cheek with her finger, as if mulling over her next move. The nail polish perfectly matched the bloodred lip color. "Relationship status?"

His cough erupted and fizzled into a nervous chuckle from her direct blast into his personal life. His lack of a current girlfriend wasn't a secret, but he was used to being in the driver's seat when testing new terrain.

"It's not a hard question." Her voice turned an edge frosty. "Unless you're about to lie."

"Single." He gulped a mouthful of beer.

"Good."

His eyebrow hitched up with his shock that she was interested in him—and for more than passing time at a party.

Problem was, and he did see it as a problem, he was interested in her, too. He cleared his throat. His body was reacting without waiting for his mind to catch up. "Are you…single?"

She nodded.

"Not that I'm trying to pick you up." He shook his head. "Commitment-phobe here. And work pretty much takes up my life." Damn. He wanted to kiss those lips, smear that color right off.

The way his body short-circuited over her, he needed to set the record straight not only for her, but mainly for him.

But now his imagination wouldn't stop its what-if scenarios. What if those long, manicured fingernails that tapped the bar's counter could one day rake along the length of his back as they lay together?

He shifted his stance, wishing he could walk off the aroused tightness in his crotch. His eyes squeezed shut as he urged his libido to get it together. Maybe he needed a double shot of oxygen to clear away these thoughts.

"You're a cop? Fireman? Navy SEAL?"

Dresden laughed and shook his head. "Professor. I teach history and write articles. Working on a book now."

"Top secret?"

"My family tree in the context of Canada's black history. I'm Canadian, by the way."

"You keep getting more interesting. Sounds like your project is a lot of work, but also eye-opening for the curious-minded."

He nodded, unable to withhold his appreciation that she showed interest in his work.

"And you haven't managed to squeeze in a significant other?"

"I have. That's how I know that it's not happening anytime soon." Despite the casual way she'd tossed out the question, he'd heard judgment.

"That's better than saying 'not in this lifetime.'"

Dresden didn't respond. While she operated as being cool and confident, he could barely keep up with his unaffected demeanor under her pointed questions.

"You gotta give a woman a teensy bit of hope or they

won't stick around to talk to you when there's a kick-butt party going on over her shoulder." A smidgen of a smile curled her lips.

Dresden got the message, but this wasn't the place to pick up anyone, even if she was rocking her tiny red mini-dress. And even if it fit like a tight glove around her curves at the top and at the bottom— He took another sip.

Reality check to self: hooking up at Grace Meadows's party couldn't happen. Shouldn't happen.

"Let me guess." She leaned toward him. He tried not to be caught in her weblike aura, but he leaned toward her. *Couldn't help it.* That damned perfume rendered him weak. "You look out at these strangers in this backdrop with doubt, maybe condemnation. I can see it on your face. You're dismissive of them for whatever reasons. That's sad. Because you're looking at me with a lot of suspicion mixed with wariness, as if I were about to suggest a one-night stand."

Dresden choked on his drink. Her boldness, her accuracy about his attraction to her, rattled his nerves. He shook his head. He'd never own up to lusting after her.

"And on that note, it's been an interesting few minutes with you, Dresden. See you around…if it's meant to be." Laxmi offered her hand once more.

This time he was prepared for the intense pleasure of holding it.

Or so he'd thought. He hadn't expected the slight squeeze of her hand before she released his with the bonus of a slow wink.

Like a magician, she flipped a business card out of her pocketbook and extended it to him from between her fingers.

"Aren't you afraid that I might use your card as a book-mark?" His voice croaked. *Must not give in.*

"Nah." Once he took the card, she continued. "I'll stay confident that you'll call."

Every part of him cheered in agreement. However, to pretend otherwise, to maintain his plan to be unavailable, thanks to her base in New York and his in Toronto, he simply slipped the card into his inside jacket pocket and picked up his drink. "Have a good night."

She was gone before he'd finished talking. Her exit had as much flair as her style. The formfitting dress left admirers—and him—gawking as she cut a path with a supermodel strut to the front of the room.

Meeting her was worth the entire night's experience. She had the unique appeal to wake him up and make him interested in something other than his current issues. Though she'd left, his system still savored the aftereffect of her energy.

Once Laxmi disappeared from his view, Dresden sighed. The fun part of the night was over. Time to grit his teeth, suck it up and formally be part of Grace Meadows's birthday bash.

Chapter 2

The music faded into the rumbling din of the guests. The clink of glass and buzz of conversation accompanied Dresden's solitary walk to the head table.

Lights suddenly dimmed over the room, wrapping everyone in soft white lights that glittered off the chandeliers. The waitstaff efficiently slipped to the perimeter of the room with dirty dishes in tow. Stage lights now brightened a wide path for the mistress of ceremonies, who'd stepped forward to take charge. Her booming voice commandeered everyone's attention as she announced that the planned program for the birthday celebration would begin.

An eager attendant, scrubbed and polished, quickly inserted himself into Dresden's space, blocking his progress to the Meadowses. "Are you part of the VIPs?" He pointed to his wrist and tapped his finger on the spot.

Dresden stared at him, clueless as to the meaning of the signal.

"VIPs have a purple bracelet. Do you have your invitation?"

Dresden nodded and showed it.

The eager and now annoyed attendant cleared his throat as he closely read the paper. "Okay. Here's your bracelet."

Dresden took the simple band and slipped it on. He squashed the stubborn urge to refuse this anointed VIP status and risk the attendant's disdain. His DNA connection to the Meadowses changed nothing. With his personal life and career pursuit solidly middle of the road, he had no experience with the airs and graces that surrounded this family.

While the emcee continued on with her introductions, he turned himself over to his escort and followed along to the head table.

"Mrs. Meadows, your guest Dresden Haynes is here." The man actually bowed. Not to a full ninety-degree angle, but enough to give deference and to earn a regal nod.

Dresden's back stiffened. She couldn't expect him to do the same? But he wasn't sure as Grace Meadows slid her keen gaze onto him. The entire table's attention followed suit, including Miss Sexy Red Dress.

Laxmi offered him an imperceptible nod. Casually posed. Neutral smile. Guess she wasn't disclosing that they'd met.

In return, he responded with a quick, dismissive nod before he turned his attention back to Grace.

"How good of you to join us," Grace said with clear imperious elocution. "I'm so thrilled that you came to my party. Now, take your seat. We are about to begin."

The woman didn't look anywhere close to eighty years old. A vibrancy burst from her like an extra ring added to her aura. Even without all the family members and the birthday decorations that framed her, she would still stand out in a crowd.

She shooed him away with a flick of her hand. "You are seated next to Fiona. Go on, take a seat."

His sister was already at his side with arms outstretched. Before he could take it all in, before he could take a step back, she pulled him into a fiercely tight hug. "I can't believe you're here. I'm so glad." Her hug grew tighter as she repeated herself.

"Good to see you, too," Dresden offered after his release from her arms. The tension interwoven through his neck muscles slackened and disappeared under her reassuring smile. During their many conversations, he'd accepted that Fiona shouldn't shoulder any blame for his lost-and-found story line. Nor should she be burdened with his pendulum swings over accepting the role and responsibilities as a Meadow or retreating to his obscurity from the family.

"Let's get the introductions over with because I'm sure your brain is on overload right now," Fiona said after he took his seat.

Her prophetic statement held true after he was reintroduced to Fiona's boyfriend, Leo; their cousins Dana and Belinda and their significant others, Kent and Jesse; and more extended family. In that last cluster of family members, he had to acknowledge Verona—Fiona's mother— the same woman who'd given him away and held on to her secret until a few months ago, when Grace and Fiona had found out about his existence.

He twisted the lock tighter on his emotions to halt any visible signs of how he felt. The order he craved in his life couldn't afford pendulum swings into drama. Neither did he want to dwell in hurt, anger or even empathy for Verona.

Feelings for this woman whom he couldn't think of as his mother didn't linger in one place. At times, he wondered about her life and the difficulty of giving him up. During those moments, he could stir up a measure of compassion without feeling any sense of obligation to talk to her. Other times, when he celebrated with his parents over the smallest joy, he could erase Verona from his conscious thoughts.

Overall, the many names he'd just learned, along with each person's identifying details, merged in a chaotic swirl of too much information. The pressure to impress, his emotions, his grudging willingness to be there, all overwhelmed him. If tested, he'd be unable to recall anything. Hopefully he wouldn't have any long conversations that would tax his memory.

But he sensed that it was an empty fantasy because their gazes stuck to him like prickly burrs. It didn't help that a few heads tilted toward each other for whispered chitchat. How much did they know about him?

"And the last one in the lineup is my friend Laxmi Holder," Fiona revealed with an appreciative pat on her friend's shoulder.

"Just to be clear, it's *best* friend." Laxmi smirked at him.

Good grief, she belongs to the other side. Dresden nodded in mock salute. "Not to worry. I won't usurp your place."

"Hope not. She's got enough friends." Laxmi pointed at Fiona with her thumb. "I, on the other hand, may have an opening for a friend with benefits." She widened her smile.

Dresden felt like her partner in crime, with their shared

secret about not being complete strangers. He swallowed the automatic response to match her smile with his. Hard to be around this intriguing woman and not react to her or anything she said. Besides, he was certain Fiona had picked up that something had occurred between the two. Although she was baffled now, no doubt that she would corner Laxmi later for the lowdown.

To throw off Fiona and get himself onto emotionally neutral land, Dresden allowed himself to drift along with the meandering conversations closest to him.

The cousins soon overshadowed his preoccupation with Laxmi. Jointly they engaged him in animated conversations exchanging information about their childhood misadventures. Listening to the details from their childhood, he felt like a spectator. He couldn't help thinking about what it would have been like to be part of the family dynamics. But their exuberance and effort to draw him in with humor and great storytelling abilities helped dissipate some of the awkwardness of the situation.

However, he took the more comfortable route to talk about his humorous interactions with his students and his more interesting research trips. Childhood stories, living in exotic places with his family, and anything else that he deemed too personal, remained unspoken.

Sliding his attention past the cousins, he saw Verona, far enough away but still in his direct line of sight. He studied the woman who'd given birth to him but couldn't look at him. She didn't smile much. Didn't talk much, either. She wasn't a sad figure. More like a contemplative spectator at the table. He wasn't sure what he'd expected or what he'd wanted—a bereaved woman in perpetual torment would be nice.

A low-level headache hummed across his brow. Maybe

he should have stayed at the bar. He needed a little help to get through the night. However, his escape plan hit a snag.

The program started with the official introduction of Grace. The matriarch walked forward to take her place on the stage. Guests cheered her on with a standing ovation. Dresden clapped along with everyone as each major accomplishment was read about her humble beginnings in the media industry to the steep upward trajectory to success and power.

He chanced a glance at Laxmi before he resumed his seat. She was chatting with one of the cousins. Not once did she look in his direction. He did but also didn't want her attention. Still, why on earth did he feel a twinge of disappointment because she ignored him?

Grace stepped up to the microphone, first acknowledging the ovation and grand introduction. Her speech turned somber and reflective.

Dresden listened to her creative version of his inclusion in the family. More details than he'd preferred, about Grace hiring Leo to find her grandson so that she could celebrate this milestone birthday with her entire family. Her pride extended to her daughter Verona and the reunion of her children, whose successful lives were testimony to the Meadowses' traits of grit and determination.

Bitterness simmered in his chest like embers. Charlotte and Patrick deserved all the credit. And he'd never betray their love by sharing any part of himself with Verona.

"Would all my grandchildren join me onstage?"

"I'm sorry. I didn't know she'd do this." Fiona touched his fisted hand on the table as she rose to join her grandmother. The cousins also stood, looking expectantly over at him.

His mind raced along with the thump of his heartbeat. His body, on the other hand, felt like it was in a high-drama family saga moving in slow motion. He had to stand. Had to walk to the stage. Had to take his place next to people he didn't know or belong with, as part of the united front for the public and for Grace.

Cameras didn't stop flashing. Were they all so fascinating, to need every facet of their life on record? He tried to shield his eyes but couldn't manage that and see to walk. Feeling more than a tad self-conscious, he retreated between a gap in the lineup. The rest of the family all dealt with it like pros.

Dresden concentrated hard on not barfing onstage. Alongside him, he witnessed Fiona, like her cousins, charm the audience with her testimonial of love and devotion for her grandmother. Their sincerity stirred up warm, cozy feelings about family and legacy. While they lauded Grace's impact to their lives, he related the same feelings to his memories of his adoptive parents. Nothing would change where his loyalty resided. Except, a deep-seated fear formed that he could fall under the spell of the Meadowses.

Meanwhile, the guests continued cheering through Fiona's speech. They were the fans for the home team, fully engaged at a pep rally. How would he follow her blaze of glory with his version as the new Meadows? What emotional bloodletting would he have to perform for the guests' satisfaction?

The anxiety had him wishing that he was back at the bar admiring a particularly sexy woman in her red-hot minidress. Timing wasn't on his side, but he'd make do with the temporary opportunity.

Damn, it was his turn. Fiona offered a final wave before she left the podium to rejoin the line of grandchildren. His nerves popped and multiplied in the pit of his belly.

Too many thoughts to process and no time for second-guessing. Dresden rubbed his palms along his pant legs and blew out a shaky breath.

The short walk to the podium felt a mile long. But nothing more delayed his face time with the guests. He tried to smile. Tried to make his face relax. Tried to hold it together.

He dug deep and imagined standing in front of a freshman class. This was nothing more than teaching the early history of Canada. If he was lucky, he'd have to deal with only a few glazed stares.

"Tonight I'm here with the Meadowses to celebrate Grace's birthday. Thank you for the invitation." He inclined his head toward the head table. "Right now…" He paused, trying to direct his words so that only positivity flowed. "This has been…quite a year." A few chuckles joined in with his weak laughter. He scratched his forehead, although there was no itch, just an unease that wouldn't stay buried. "A lot to take in. And we will move onward and upward. So, um…enjoy the meal."

Then he took a step back from the podium. With a loud exhalation, he looked over at Fiona. *Sorry.* He mouthed the word before looking back out over the crowd. A soft buzz of chatter gradually filled in the silence after he finished.

He sought one person's judgment—Laxmi's. He was sure Grace regretted his stumbling debut to her friends. That was why he'd rather deal with Laxmi and her series of pointed questions about his behavior than Fiona's or Grace's disappointment.

Without pausing to analyze the consequences of the next steps, Dresden walked briskly off the stage. His strides lengthened and picked up momentum toward the exit. Escape. Freedom. All he wanted right now was cool air filling his lungs.

He reached the hotel entrance out of breath, but grateful, and pushed open the door. The temperature had dropped significantly, adding a frigid edge to the already frosty condition. His face tightened against the wind but he needed the briskness to take his mind off his actions.

"Sir, do you need a taxi?" An attendant stepped up, ready to hail a cab with his whistle.

"I guess I should get one." Dresden looked around for the limo. He'd gotten out of the vehicle without ensuring that he had a ride after the party. And there was no sign of the car or driver.

"That won't be necessary. I'll take the runaway to his hotel."

The attendant nodded and left him at the curb.

Dresden slowly turned in the direction of Laxmi's voice. She greeted him with a cocky smirk and headed over to the valet service booth. A red coat shielded her body against the cold. Like the red dress, the perfectly matched coat complemented her skin. And, oh, man, that strut she had was always a pleasure to watch.

First, he didn't know if he wanted to be rescued. Second, should she be his knight in a hot minidress? But he didn't want to ponder the dilemmas for any real answer.

A spectacular red Ferrari Sergio roared into view and pulled up beside them. Dresden watched Laxmi tip the valet before sliding behind the steering wheel.

Did she plan for every part of her life to be in sync? The sports car matched its owner—brash and eye-catching with compelling power moves. As she fluffed out her hair and let it fall past her shoulders in a thick, curly black curtain, he knew she had the "it" factor for an expensive car ad.

"Oh, come on. I'm harmless." The limited-edition

roadster's engine revved like a signal for him to get in and enjoy the ride.

"I'm not supposed to take rides from strangers." He tried not to fall under her spell. All night he had tried, but as his hand closed on the door handle, he knew he couldn't go on unless he surrendered to this woman.

An exciting shiver ran along his spine. She pressed a red lipstick to her bottom lip and smoothed on a fresh coat. He followed its path over the curves and valley of her lips. To survive the moment, he looked around for a distraction.

Seeing the valet looking longingly at the car instead of drooling over Laxmi worked for Dresden. Not that he could claim to be jealous of someone he didn't know.

"Didn't envision this gem as my getaway car." He got into the tight space and pushed back his seat to match hers.

"And I never imagined that I'd be racing off with such a worthy prize."

"Prize? Guess that's what I am…to them." He looked toward the entrance. The way he'd left, the things he'd said or hadn't said—all of it ran on a continuous loop. There was no coming back from this. Should he never have said yes to Fiona's invite? Now he'd made a mess of things and embarrassed Grace on her birthday. He swore under his breath.

"Want to head back in?"

"No. Actually, I did what I came to do. No more. No less." He shrugged off the denial that popped up.

"At least sleep on it. You might think differently in the morning."

"Are you the getaway driver or my therapist?" So what if he sounded ungrateful?

Laxmi didn't consider herself the most observant person. Her client, Tonea, tended to accuse her of being clueless most of the time. Tonight was one of the occasions when clarity arrived and stuck around long enough for her to pay attention to her new drinking buddy—Dresden, the missing Meadows.

She sensed that he had been equally nervous about attending the party, of course, for different reasons. His reluctance to engage was understandable, but also a welcome distraction. Plus, he was so darn fine that she couldn't resist flirting.

But when he went onstage, she saw the panic. She recognized the signs of feeling out of control, looking out at the crowd for approval and hoping to impress. His panic got the better of him and he bolted.

As soon as he left the stage, Laxmi shot out of her seat and followed. Maybe she was looking for an excuse to also leave, but there was a part of her that was genuinely interested in Dresden.

Even if he met her concern with full-out suspicion.

"I'm Fiona's friend. So, she matters and, by default, you matter."

"Then let me relieve you of that obligation." He reached for the door handle.

But his head hit the headrest as Laxmi pushed the gas pedal. Tires squealed. Pedestrians skipped out of the way, hopping onto the curb. Their departure from the front of the hotel turned into a blurred flash of buildings and lights.

Not until Laxmi pulled up at a red light did Dresden test the seat belt. He kept one hand on the dashboard for added measure as she took off again. A sharp right turn tested his grip on every surface. A side glance to check on Laxmi only proved that the ride to his hotel would feel like a jump through a time warp.

"Where to?" she asked in between a three-lane change.

"I chose to stay at the Barkley Towers."

"Nice digs. Everyone is at the Winthorpe."

"I know," he said. Fiona had offered to make the reservation at the same hotel, but he'd known he'd need his space. Besides, he'd passed on the Meadowses picking up the tab for his hotel stay.

"You're a loner? Not judging." Her hand rose against his instant protest. "Call me being observant."

She banked a hard left. A few car horns blasted their owners' annoyance. With another squeal of brakes, they pulled up in front of the hotel, a much quieter venue than the location for the birthday bash.

"Home sweet home."

"Thanks." Dresden unsnapped the seat belt and opened the car door. "I really appreciate...this."

"No problem. My pleasure."

He looked up at the building, glad to be in his safe space. Yet he didn't want to part ways with Laxmi. "You've missed a lot of the festivities. Sorry about that."

"Yes, but then, you wouldn't have been there. Who would I have spent my time getting to know?" She shook her head. "Nah. I'm in the right place at the right time."

"Do you want to come in for a drink?" He plunged ahead without bothering to have a comeback if she rejected him.

"Oh. I'm shocked." She clearly teased him. "Didn't think you were into one-night stands." Her audacious wink drew his laughter.

"I promise that no such thing will occur."

"Bummer." She emerged from the car and handed over the keys to the valet. "And here I thought you were going to be interesting."

Dresden didn't know how to deal with his unlikely

partner in crime. They walked into the lobby, with her hand tucked into the crook of his elbow, and then stepped onto the elevator. She hummed a tune he didn't recognize. He looked straight ahead, hoping she couldn't see his heart popping out of his chest, pumping like an overworked piston.

As soon as the doors opened and they stepped into the hallway, Laxmi said, "Somehow I pictured you in a setting like this."

"Old and dusty?" He didn't think she was laying down a compliment.

"An appreciation of the old mixed with the new. You're a history professor. But you also have written some interesting articles on various topics with a predictive air about what the future holds. How the past doesn't have to dictate the future. In other words, you are an optimist."

Laxmi once had been an optimist. The high ledge where hope and ideals resided was for those lucky souls. But the space had felt narrow and uncomfortable once her life unraveled with loss and defeat.

Maybe her attraction to Dresden began with his air of optimism. Why else would he attend Grace's party, despite his hasty departure?

"You knew who I was?"

"Not right away. Although, Dresden is an unusual name. But the aha moment hit when you showed up at the table."

Dresden groaned. He didn't want to remember his most recent personal history. He slid the hotel key card into the lock and motioned for her to enter.

"You know once I cross the threshold, you've officially invited me in."

"And I'm all out of garlic and holy water."

"I won't put any moves on you."

The declaration disappointed him. He was too damned ready to wrap his arms around her fine body and deliver a long, hard kiss.

"Oh, what the hell." She grabbed his shirt and pulled him to her. "No?" She licked her lips. "Or yes?"

"Hell, yes." He kissed her just the way he'd imagined the sensation of falling backward into bliss without knowing how far beneath him the bottom was.

Chapter 3

Laxmi held on for dear life, or more accurately, for the sheer enjoyment of being in Dresden's arms. All night she'd engaged in sexy fantasies about kissing him. Getting herself hot and stirring up her desire weren't anywhere on her party agenda, but she hadn't expected her evening to turn into a night of interesting diversions.

Not only didn't she expect to run into the missing heir from the Meadows family tree at the bar, not that she'd been on the lookout, but her imagination could have never come up with this end result.

Now she could barely breathe as they devoured each other. Her arms clasped tighter around his shoulders. She sucked in gulps of air while his lips roughly ravished hers.

"You're freaking delicious," she whispered. Delicious to taste, see, smell. She inhaled the masculine notes of his cologne.

"Likewise, my knight to the rescue." His deep, rumbly voice stroked in all the right places.

Hungry and ready, she held on and wrapped her legs around his hips. Her head was buried against his neck, along his cheek, until her mouth reconnected again to his sweet desperation.

The more they kissed, the more she didn't want it to end. All of this, all of him, felt right and beautiful. She pressed her body against his, holding on, succumbing to his kisses peppering her chest.

Her eyes fluttered open as she sank onto his bed.

He loomed over her, out of breath, wearing his shy smile that had knocked her off balance when she'd first seen him at the bar.

His eyes couldn't mask his feelings, though. They communicated on full blast with what turned him on, turned him off, or what left him pensive, such as when he was onstage with the rest of the Meadowses. His deep brown eyes surely served as his soul's windows.

"So what now?" she asked in a deliberate offhand manner.

He sucked on her thumb that still lingered on the cushiony softness of his lips. Her desire shot through her body and pooled between her legs like a hungry snake coiling and ready to be satisfied.

"I don't do one-night stands." His hand cupped her breast, taking possession. Under the continuous stroke of his thumb, her sensitive nipple perked against the attention.

"Neither do I." She licked her lips, hoping for another serving of his tongue to sweep hers into a sexy tango.

"Good. We're in agreement." His hand slid up her dress and pulled her thong down her legs before he tossed it aside.

"Just make sure that it's not a one-nighter." She eyed the red thong hanging off the lampshade next to the bed. "I'll definitely need a repeat of you," she said, almost as if giving herself a necessary reminder.

His hands slid under her body and worked the zipper down her back.

"You'll have to peel me out of this outfit." She giggled as she remembered how she'd shimmied in place to get dressed.

"Looking forward to it," he said. His fingers teased her skin as he unwrapped the dress from around her body.

Goose bumps prickled her arms with anticipation and as reward for the casual brush of his hands around her waist and along her hips.

Strong, yet gentle, his fingertip traced symbols of infinity along her flesh. She hoped he never stopped. Her moans partnered with her body, which was writhing under the attention. Pleasurable shivers shimmied through her.

"Getting you out of my system may take a little while." Laxmi couldn't help confessing her inner thoughts to this man.

"Same here." He kissed the edge of her shoulder where a monarch-butterfly tattoo imprinted her skin. The colorful charm served her well as a reminder of having faith after her darkest days.

"Wasn't supposed to happen this way," she whispered, giving voice to the argument within her.

His focused expression softened with a hint of a smile. Maybe he agreed.

The smile turned her on. Discovering every feature excited her. She traced a line from his forehead over his nose and the spread of his nostrils. A soft sweep of his lips with her thumb paid homage to a key feature she'd instantly fallen for earlier that evening.

He unbuttoned his shirt, but she couldn't stay patient for his intentional performance of slowly undressing. While he dealt with that, she unfastened his pants and assisted him out of them with such vigor that they collapsed into each other's arms, both laughing heartily.

Once they'd restored order with her blushing and him clearing his throat, she had to admit to wanting all the time to look at his naked body.

"Maybe we should exchange some sort of pleasantries."

"Now?" Laxmi couldn't curb the fit of giggles as Dresden leaned against the wall with too much casualness. She didn't want to deal with any speed bumps slowing the momentum of a spectacular nightcap.

He kissed her pout until her lips relaxed and welcomed his mouth and the bold stroke of his tongue. *Damn, he can kiss.* She wrapped her legs around him to wipe out any gaps between them.

"You know, to make this less of a booty call." He nuzzled her neckline, tracing the curve to her shoulders.

"Aw, you're sweet," she teased. "Okay, then let's go with word association. You get five words and I get five. One-word questions and answers." She grasped his firm behind in her hands and stroked the thick hardness of muscle.

"Home?" he asked through clenched teeth to begin the game.

"Brooklyn." Her hands stroked upward along the contour of his back. "Your mom's basement?"

He laughed and handily took possession of her hands above her head. "Heck no. And that's three words." He punished her with a series of wet kisses around her nipple. "Canada?" he prompted. Meanwhile he continued teasing the valley between her breasts.

She arched up for more of his tongue's wickedness. "Doable." Talking and moaning almost made her words unintelligible. She could barely think. "Purse," she hissed.

"It's my turn. Gosh, you cheat." He nuzzled her earlobe, which might as well be a turn-up-the-dial on the heat in her.

"Purse," she repeated with a gasp.

"Red."

"No." She pointed to the tiny accessory abandoned on the hotel desk.

He shook his head, looking confused.

She giggled. "I meant for you to hand me my purse. Condoms."

"Smart." He nodded.

"They are in my purse." She couldn't stop laughing at him.

"I take it we're done with the games." He handed her the small red purse.

"Pretty much." She pulled out the condom and ripped the packet apart.

"I'll do it. You may tip me over before I'm ready." He plucked the condom from her fingers.

Dresden the history professor and Dresden the one-night-stand lover boy didn't compute. But this onetime scenario happened when he tucked logic away like a pesky friend.

From his departure from the party to the arrival at this hotel room with Laxmi, he'd sailed through his experiences with the rush of adrenaline going through his veins. He was open to every sensation and Laxmi delivered, keeping all his senses on high alert.

Yet he regretted nothing, instead diving into the deep end and enjoying whatever happened between in this moment. He had no misguided supposition that there would an episodic drama after this night. She'd made it clear that she was operating on satisfying a whim. And he had no desire to ignite anything that asked for commitment or long term.

His plate was pretty full with the Meadowses.

And he wanted to forget them, if only for a little while.

Laxmi watched him prep himself.

Raw hunger fueled her desire. The man certainly could send her into a swoon. He was simply beautiful. The naked statues of male Greek gods in the museums all over the world had nothing on him. While those physiques were born of a sculptor's imagination, this man was blessed with natural strength, power and lean muscular build.

The lights hadn't been dimmed. A consideration she appreciated for the juicy privilege of watching him walk toward her. No shadowy darkness shielded him from her view. Smooth skin, rich with color, stoked her desire to touch him. An appetite for him to pleasure her grew with a deep gnawing as if it was an actual hunger pang craving nourishment.

No other way to admit that she'd fallen under his spell, even if he hadn't cast one. His loner personality tugged at her interest. His body tugged on a lot more. She was so wet as her gaze lapped him up to feed her soul.

She shifted her eyes from his erection to look in his eyes. Her cheeks remained warm when she saw that he was aware of her appreciation.

"I don't want you to think that I'm rushing things." His tone questioned her.

She shook her head. If he knew of her turmoil, the giddy sensation of being twirled around a room and let go, he might not believe her. But she loved the free fall from the dizzying height of her current situation. Maybe that need to take risks continued to guide her, pushing her toward independence and challenging her to step out of her comfort zone. Being around Dresden shook her world in a good way. He wasn't the average man. This wasn't the average hookup.

"Good." His mouth closed over a nipple and his tongue played with the taut nub. Then his head popped up. "'Cause I'm having the time of my life with you."

Laxmi softly clasped his head between her hands and pulled him to her mouth for a kiss. His consideration touched her. She tried not to jump ahead and contemplate when they'd have to go their separate ways. She was adult enough to know that any promises made to each other in the heat of the moment didn't mean they would be honored. After all, an internationally recognized border stood between them.

It is a fact of life. She couldn't open her heart for a what-if moment. *Stay focused.* Her mission was to prove that she could climb back to the successful side of the entertainment world after a failed singing career. She'd already placed hazard warnings around her heart for any failed attempts at true love.

This night could never be repeated, despite how much she wanted another chance to feel wanted and desired by a real man.

Despite the practical advisory, the reality carried a sting.

"Don't get quiet on me," he whispered with his forehead pressed against hers.

"Does this look quiet to you?" She leaned back on her elbows.

He growled, deep and guttural. They were done talking.

She barely had time to grab hold of him as he scooped her up and brought their hips for a momentous meet-up. She welcomed all of him, grinding against his pelvis.

They moved as one, neither wanting to let go. From the bed, to the floor, to the chair, to the wall, Laxmi crawled, writhed and rolled around with Dresden deep within her.

Life felt good.

He felt good.

Her back stayed pressed against the cold, hard bedroom wall, to keep her upright, but also to keep her in place for Dresden's rhythmic thrusts.

She kept her eyes closed. Listening to his grunts ramped up her need for him to fill her even more. Over and over again.

"Hold on." His command sounded like a voice-over for the unfolding action.

She obeyed without needing any prompt. Her cheek pressed against the soft waves of his hair. She held on so tight that she was sure her cheek would show the imprint of his hair.

Reading her readiness, he slowed, sliding into her with deliberate pressure and pulling out for her to enjoy every glorious part. At the peak, she let go and let her body release, pulsate until she was done.

Gripping his shoulders, she stayed perched around his hips. As he picked up the pace to thrust into her, he came hard. And she thanked her luck that she'd met this wonderful man tonight.

They finally had touched down and coasted back to reality. Only their uneven breaths added sound to the silence. Within each other's embrace, they ushered in a calm, reflective mood after their steamy, passionate union.

"Whew," Laxmi said to ward off the onset of nerves. "I would say let's go for round two, but a girl's got a business to run." She slid along the wall to free herself and her mind from Dresden's proximity.

"And I've got a plane to catch in a few hours." He looked at his watch and didn't look her way again.

"I'll just step into the bathroom." Laxmi straightened her clothes and headed for the door.

Dresden released a breath when the bathroom door closed. If he was hooked up to diagnostic machines, the readout would be haphazard. Emotions and hard thinking battled for his mind's forefront.

Never having been high, he imagined this floating sensation and craving for more must come pretty close. But the changes in him weren't only physical. That scared him. The shift toward wanting Laxmi, wanting to be friends, wanting more than that, was too swift. He didn't operate on impulse. Well, up to a few minutes ago, he'd have made that claim.

But her kick-ass style and fearless approach stirred desire. He wanted the time to get to know her. And he hoped that she'd let him convince her that he was worth the effort.

Behind the closed door, in much-needed privacy, she cleaned up while her mind scrolled through a panicked stream of thoughts. A ragged edge of self-doubt gnawed at her confidence. If she hadn't pushed her way into Dresden's space, would he have been interested? She knew the answer, as she leaned in to the mirror, peering at her reflection as if it was an out-of-body experience. So far tonight, she had walked on the wild side, but was still uncertain about how the final credits would roll. Unplanned moments had a tendency to go haywire. Right now, her emotions were running ahead of her logic, looking to escape.

Was she the bad guy? Cut and run and never look back. Or could she play the good girl? Diplomatic and vague, but still run. Her past was her being the naive woman hanging on too long to a bad apple. She'd played at being cavalier with Dresden. But the plan had backfired. She was far from unaffected by Dresden. Too dangerous to her willpower. A fast retreat was necessary.

Laxmi reapplied her lipstick, dabbed at the sheen on her forehead and smoothed her hair back into place, as much as possible. A twist here and a turn there, she finished the inspection on her clothes. Her thong. Still on the lampshade. Time to head back out there and act like she wasn't a case of nerves.

No matter how she felt, she didn't wish him to be constrained by her insecurities. Keep things simple and not emo-girl whiny. Taking deep breaths in and out, Laxmi was ready to play the role of independent, emotionally detached young woman.

At first she didn't see or hear him when she emerged from the bathroom. Even if he was inclined, there weren't too many places to jump out and scare her. Anyway, she hurried over to the side table and grabbed her underwear. She'd just pulled her dress down when the sound of a key card activating the door stopped her plan to search for him behind the thick drapes.

"I bought a couple sodas." He handed her a cold Coke. His eyes shifted from around the room to her outstretched hand, but never to her face.

Was he feeling regret? Shame? Or was he in need of closure?

"Thanks. That's thoughtful." She didn't drink sodas, but the correction didn't matter. Her fingers brushed along his—deliberate on her part. She wanted contact and a signal that nothing would be awkward. Still he didn't bring his gaze back to her. Things would be awkward.

"Did you need anything else?" He motioned with his chin toward the bathroom.

"I'm good." Why did he have to look all pulled together? Meanwhile, a few minutes ago, her hair had sported a bad case of bed-head. Smeared lipstick had given her the clown-mouth effect. And her skin had appeared dewy from the naturally sweaty workout.

Not fair.

Laxmi grabbed her keys and pocketbook. She took a pass on offering her hand for a shake or tiptoeing to meet his lips for a kiss. Instead she said, "Hope everything works out for you. If you're ever in the city, you have my card."

She hurriedly opened the door and stepped into the hallway, praying it would quickly swing shut. She sounded like a handyman hoping for a call back after tackling a problem.

"Wait. I'll walk with you."

"Not necessary." She sped up her retreat to the elevator. "I'm in a rush."

His unhurried footsteps followed her quick strides. She turned the corner to the bank of elevators, ready to summon one. The longer she stayed in this building, the more trapped she felt. Fresh air would help a lot. She waited with a small huddle of hotel guests, hoping that the elevator arrived before Dresden.

But he appeared around the corner, still unhurried, not

breathing as if he had to catch up to the finish line, unlike her heaving chest. Maybe he recognized the lack of privacy, because he said nothing, his face a stoic mask. Instead he stood next to her, joining everyone's stance to stare at the numbers above the elevator as it moved up or down.

Finally a chime behind them indicated a door would open. Laxmi waited for the family of four to board the space before she stepped in and faced front, while Dresden followed suit.

The other guests continued with their conversation, which helped to make the ride down slightly bearable.

"You really didn't have to come with me," she whispered.

"You've made that clear."

He sounded annoyed.

The door opened and Laxmi almost tumbled out, glad to be free from the confining space. Now that the exit wasn't far from where she stood, her equilibrium righted to stiffen her spine.

"Why are you running?" His attention stayed with the flow of foot traffic coming and going through the entrance.

"I'm not. It's just time for me to go." She didn't slow down as she headed through the doors and requested her car.

"And I thought that I was the one to run." He barely smiled at his joke.

"If I stay, we'd be breaking our pact to remain uninvolved. This wasn't supposed to happen. I came to a birthday party to hang out with my friend and catch up on our years apart while eating birthday cake. And you were going to be introduced to Grace's circle." She stepped off the curb to head for her car that had pulled up. "We were the anomaly of the evening."

"I have no complaints." He remained on the curb.

She looked over the top of the car at him. "Neither do I."

"Well, break the rule. Let's do this." His suggestion touched her like the gentleness of his hand cupping her face.

She looked up at the dark night, unable to see any stars. Bright city lights illuminated the steep heights of the buildings. Once upon a time, she had broken lots of rules, done things her way, and had a lot to be sorry for in the process.

Dresden hadn't moved or changed his expression. Still the handsome guy who'd caught her eye. Did he understand the consequences of tossing out that temptation as a finale for the night?

"Let's end on a high note." She got into her car before he responded and before she changed her mind.

Her passenger door opened. Dresden leaned in. "Maybe we're more alike than you think. And—"

"No." She shook her head for added emphasis. "You're in Canada. I'm in New York."

"There's such a thing called planes."

"I'm in entertainment—it's a hustle. There's no time for dating or thinking about you. I go where the business takes me. I can barely look after me. I don't want—"

"I don't need to be looked after. And life is a hustle that we don't always get right."

Laxmi stared straight ahead. She had to erase his words of hope, his expectant look, the memory of what that mouth had delivered on her body. She bit her lip to add a stinging reminder to get it together.

"I don't have what you're looking for. I'm not the girlfriend who could be counted on to be reliable or dependable." Laxmi revved the engine. "But one day you will find that special someone because you're a nice guy and you'll see that this wasn't it."

"I'll let you go…for now." He stepped back and closed the car door.

Laxmi snapped on her seat belt, glanced into the side mirror for oncoming traffic and pushed down on the gas. She needed the city's frenetic driving scene to harness her attention.

For now.
For now?

Chapter 4

Monday promised to feel like the worst hangover Laxmi had ever had without alcohol involved. Insomnia hit two nights in a row, marching in like a tuba player blowing his way into a library. Wide-awake and consumed with Dresden aptly described those sleepless hours. Dreams of him lingered, infusing her thoughts with sexy images of him and playing X-rated loops of him satisfying her. Even now her cheeks warmed under the memory of his actions and her reactions.

Despite her half-hearted plan-A attempt to push the memories off-road, she'd come up with plan B: a late-night, full-blast treadmill run to make her crash from exhaustion into bed. That didn't help.

Binge-watching TV show marathons of *Empire* and *Power* failed, too. Like it was a bad cold, she'd have to let whatever had overcome her run its course until she could get through at least one hour without sighing like a young girl with a crush.

Added to her anxiety was her packed calendar, guaranteed to keep her hopping around New York with a few extended trips. Managing an up-and-coming music artist required patience for the long phase of planting seeds. Mostly the effort drained resources and energy with unbelievable time-suck for promotions. But the breakthrough, just one sliver of light in the seemingly thick darkness, would materialize from one of those wildly tossed seeds on a bleak landscape.

Today, at this very moment, would not be the day for career breakthroughs. After talking to Fiona briefly on the phone, her friend popped up at the recording studio, where Laxmi waited for Tonea's arrival. The curt conversation clued Laxmi in that Fiona wasn't happy. She didn't have to guess what troubled Fiona since it was only the second day since the birthday party and Dresden's epic departure.

"Laxmi, stop pretending to tune me out. I know you've heard every word."

"Huh?" Laxmi looked up from the control board and over at Fiona, who marched back and forth in the tight space.

Her friend stopped and put her hands on her hips. "No one leaves Grace's events. First Dresden left. Then you were gone. At least he called to apologize."

"I called your grandmother and promised my first-born," Laxmi clarified half-jokingly.

"But you didn't call me. And I called you several times." Fiona pushed Laxmi's chair with her foot until it swiveled and they faced each other. "Well…?"

"You wouldn't have let me apologize over the phone. And all my emails about meeting for coffee and a quick chat went unanswered." Laxmi diverted her attention by scrolling through the calendar on her phone. Better to keep Fiona's keen investigative powers from detecting any part she'd played in Dresden's disappearance.

"I was mad, dammit. And I don't need any more mysteries about my bro—Dresden—to solve. I've got a couple unrelated cases about missing teens sitting on my desk."

"Hello…you're on vacation. And there's no mystery to solve about your brother."

"Well, it's killing me not to be in the office. I'm heading home tonight."

"And Leo?" Laxmi had talked to Fiona's boyfriend for only a few minutes. They looked madly in love and he was quite popular with her cousins and their significant others.

"He's sticking around Manhattan to deal with Grace's business."

Laxmi laughed. "Despite all your whining about your grandmother's stranglehold on the family, you had to hook up with her lawyer."

"Estate lawyer. One of many. And 'stranglehold' is an overstatement by a fragile teenager." Fiona grinned, breaking free of the moody attitude.

"Leo seems like a very nice guy and looks really comfortable with your family."

"He is, on both counts."

"Love has certainly given you a bloom."

"Shut up." Fiona smacked Laxmi's shoulder. The sappy smile was beyond cute.

"Not lying or teasing you. Really, you look happy, contented. Glad you found your special someone."

The conversation drifted into silence. Laxmi hoped that she didn't sound wistful. She had no intention of falling off that cliff again. Some people were meant to be alone and enjoy their company without an apology for the single life.

"I hope you'll stick around." Fiona looked hopeful. "We've got a lot of catching up to do. And you're always welcome at my house for an old-fashioned slumber party."

"Yeah, I'd like that. Once I get everything to a point that I can relax, a quick getaway to your upstate New York paradise sounds like a plan."

"I'll hold you to it."

"So tell me what you're working on for work." Laxmi hadn't forgotten the initial reason for Fiona's visit. Coaxing her to her happy place might minimize how much she gnashed her teeth when she eventually told Fiona the details of Saturday night, minus a few necessary deletions.

"Everyone is treating the latest case as the classic teenage runaway story—dysfunctional family history, mixed up with a bad crowd, or spoiled and wants attention. But I'm not feeling that any of those scenarios paint a complete picture. Some details don't add up." Fiona blew out a frustrated sigh. "Budget cuts don't help matters, either."

Laxmi always admired her friend for sticking with the job of her heart. To see her ready to dive into the messiest of cases both scared and thrilled her. Nothing remotely dangerous had ever held any fascination for Laxmi.

But when she'd met Fiona in college, they'd hit it off immediately. However, Los Angeles had become the go-to place for what Laxmi had wanted to do. A dream to be a singer and maybe act on the side drove her to the place where millions also chased the chance for a break.

That break came so suddenly and left just as quickly that she'd barely had time to register the accolades and the awards. "One-hit wonder" became her label with the additional descriptor of "an overnight success." As if all the work she had put in and the road leading up to that moment had been discounted.

Bit by bit, rejection after rejection, Laxmi had grown tired of the game. She was no longer relevant. And racing to catch up was similar to a hamster on a wheel.

Anger and bitter disappointment had grabbed her by the hand and taken her down some roads that never should be traveled. She remembered Fiona reaching out to her many times, trying to reconnect. The memory of her scornful reaction to her friend's helping hand still shamed her.

Her jealousy, which had blossomed like poison ivy during that time, had driven a wedge between them. She'd deemed it unfair that her journey had never lifted off beyond a certain point with temporary financial success, while Fiona had the safety net of the Meadows name and wealth behind her, regardless of whether she failed at her job. She'd never understood why Fiona wanted to hang on to their friendship.

"You know I always wanted to be you." Fiona's laughter filled the studio.

"Good grief, why?" Laxmi waved off Fiona's protests.

"Really. You had spunk. To leave home and venture out in the unknown showed independence and your bad-ass mind-set."

"'Bad' pretty much sums it up."

Fiona shook her head. "If you'd stayed in Virginia after college, you wouldn't have built up the stamina that you've got to do all of this. You're a survivor."

"It's called paying the bills."

"You can downplay it all you want. But I came to several concerts. I saw how you interacted with your fans. I heard that voice, too. Special. Unique. Hadn't reached its fullest potential."

"What?" Laxmi hadn't thought Fiona's interest went beyond casual support of her music. "Why didn't you let me know?"

Fiona shrugged. "Guess I was a teensy bit jealous. You looked great onstage. Fans screamed your name. You were gorgeous, famous and living your dream."

"Makeup and lighting, honey, do wonders. And hardly famous. Maybe two people knew me on sight." Laxmi nudged her. Compliments embarrassed her and she preferred hiding behind an air of indifference. "Anyway, I would've loved to see you there."

"Yeah, my maturity was at the ground-floor level. So much time wasted on small stuff. Taking a page from Grace's philosophy. No do-overs. Pull up your big-girl panties and move your behind toward your happiness. Friends forever."

"Friends forever," Laxmi echoed before Fiona crashed into her with a tight hug.

When Fiona released her, she said, "You look great sitting on the other side of the booth." Fiona pulled up the chair next to hers and played with the various knobs on the board. "You're like the captain of a starship."

Whether because she had the mark of a survivor or the brand of someone too stubborn to know when she was out of the game, Laxmi had emerged from her personal hell of professional failure and bad boyfriends who either used her as a stepping-stone to get into the business or wanted to introduce her to the seedy side to give her street cred for her too-clean image. All she wanted from a man, her man, was a decent, loving person who wasn't constantly challenged to be honest and respectful.

Fiona's occasional text messages had always seemed to come through at the right time to boost her out of the doldrums.

Now Laxmi wanted to help someone with the same dream, but guide them around or through the pitfalls lying in wait on the path to success. She'd connected with Tonea Brandywine, her one and only client, who was the opposite of her—a young woman with a supportive family who pursued her life's dream. Quite unlike her own personal story of going it alone without her mother's blessing and using her career pursuit as her escape, more than her deep-seated desire. But whatever forces drew them together, she and Tonea were on this journey.

"Thanks for the vote of confidence. It's a little scary, though, when Tonea is looking back at me for approval or for a measured critique." She paused to look at the empty space with the bar stool and microphone. Her pulse ticked up a notch just thinking about her client's expectations. "What if I'm wrong?"

"I think the way it works is that we'll never be always right. But if we can get our decisions and actions to be on point more often than not, then we're moving in the right direction. Have faith. Cut yourself some slack. You've got this."

"Always the cheerleader," Laxmi teased.

"Bite your tongue. I'm hardly the cheery optimist. But I know that you've got something special here with your management business and this young woman."

Laxmi nodded. It was that elusive touch of magic she had once experienced that set her in motion once again.

Fiona was right. Returning home to New York was the beginning of her redemption. Together with Tonea, who was from Atlanta, they would make their mark. And reconnecting with Fiona was also a necessity for healing. All the fences she'd resurrected in anger and ego needed tearing down; terrain needed mending and rebuilding. Good intentions held no guarantees. She had to fight the frequent urge to escape when life demanded more than she had to give. Shutting out people, especially those close to her, was a learned, well-honed habit from her life.

Her mother, the ice queen of relationships, mostly with her daughter, had forced her hand to make her head for California.

The state's warmth had thawed the frosted, barren conditions of Laxmi's soul. Out there, unfettered by her mother's negative judgment usually stoked by too much bourbon and loathing of her daughter's existence, Laxmi fed greedily on anyone's attention. And as for her father, he'd been MIA from her life way before she could form a memory or bond.

Those willing to take her hand saw the naïveté and desperation, and sucked her dry. In between the dismantling of her identity, her singing success emerged like a seedling, looking for light and sustenance. Bitter and proud, a lethal combination, she'd climbed the charts, listened to no one and given her appetite for wild partying a free rein. For those hours, she'd ward off her mother's words echoing deep within her, she'd push down on the fear of the blind curve just on the horizon, and she could pretend that she had a room filled with people who genuinely liked her—not the singer, but her.

But success packed its bags and left. No lingering goodbyes. No signs of a return. It departed and slammed the door closed behind it. The tumble wasn't a slow roll but a downward spiral that picked up momentum. The people who were her so-called friends moved out of the way for the fall and disappeared for the aftermath.

Laxmi bit her lip and then plunged ahead. She'd do whatever she had to for this friendship. "And I'm sorry for skipping out of the birthday celebration. I'd gone after Dresden."

"Why?" Fiona's tone matched the sudden shift in her expression. The detective was in action.

"I saw his reaction onstage, just before he abruptly left. He was upset. Maybe he needed a friendly ear. I've been to numerous family events when things go south."

"But nothing was going south. It was only a birthday party."

"Maybe for you. Not for him." Oooh, maybe she shouldn't have snapped that response. Laxmi didn't need to be a keen-eyed detective to read the scowl on her friend's face.

"And you know what he's thinking?"

Laxmi didn't respond as quickly because she really didn't know. In the harsh light of the present without dimmed lights, the festive mood and secret, flirtatious glances, she could only admit that she'd guessed what he'd thought or felt. "No. Not really."

"Nevertheless, you judged and inserted yourself."

"Whoa, a bit harsh. We'd met at the bar before he came to the table and—"

"I knew it," Fiona exclaimed. "I'd picked up on something between you and him at the table. The secret glances. Soft smiles. I bet if you were sitting closer together, you'd be playing footsie under the table."

Laxmi didn't know how to answer. "We met at the bar on the way to the table. Why does it sound like a World War Three moment?"

Fiona waved off her question. "So you ran off with him. Then what?"

"I didn't intend to run off with him. I asked if he needed a ride. He looked stranded. I had my car, so…" Laxmi assuaged any guilty feelings with technicalities. She hadn't calculated or planned her night with Dresden. She'd simply seized an opportunity.

"He got in your car?"

"Yeah." Laxmi leaned back in her chair and matched Fiona's folded arms. Fully irritated with the direction of the interrogation, she refused to fold under her friend's tactics.

"And you drove him to…your place?" Fiona's icy gaze did have a way of expertly sending its chilly message.

"I took him to his hotel." Before her friend could spout like a geyser, Laxmi asked, "That's a problem?"

Fiona's frown deepened. For the first time after the turn of the conversation, her friend didn't meet Laxmi's eyes.

"Hooking up with Dresden. Is that a problem?" Laxmi homed in on what she suspected was the issue. A part of her knew the answer while still wanting to hear otherwise.

"It wouldn't be a problem."

"Okay." Laxmi exhaled and sat back.

"It wouldn't be a problem because you wouldn't go down that road. You shouldn't."

The warning grazed like a bullet that nearly missed her heart.

Fiona continued. "Dresden and I are still working out the entire situation. And while he may have strong feelings about it all, I see him as a brother. A brother who needs to be protected from the media. I don't want him used because he's a Meadows or hunted by reporters for his reaction."

"Stop right there. You're making it sound like I'm a part of the great unwashed—those paparazzi jerks. And, for the record, he's an adult. Has been for a while. Long before the Meadowses popped into his life to pull him into the fold." Laxmi stopped and exhaled. "Sorry about that. I think we just should leave it here." Laxmi didn't mind retreating to save their fragile reunion.

"No, let's get everything out in the open. I'm all about speaking my mind. I didn't know how much I cared about the family legacy until I saw my cousins work hard to be a part of the Meadowses' tradition yet still be independent. But it took seeing Leo work on my grandmother's wish to reunite all of us that I realized what we have as a family is more important than what's out there, always ready to knock us down or rip us apart."

"That's not me." Laxmi hoped that Fiona didn't include her in that wide sweep.

Fiona didn't reassure her as she continued, "I know that Dresden needs the time and space to get to know us and hopefully have some type of relationship with our mother. That's my wish." Fiona's voice dropped low and soft with her closing thought. "You might not understand what it's like to have an important bond with a mother."

Laxmi cleared her throat. She wasn't prone to giving emotional speeches, but she heard the pain and hope in Fiona's message. But she also heard an accusation leveled against her that didn't sit well in her gut. "He has a mother." She stared back at Fiona until she visibly retreated from that fight. "And tell me, how am I going to disrupt your plans?"

"Disrupt should be more like delay. To have Dresden caught up with you would take him off track."

"Me in particular or any woman?"

"I probably wouldn't have this conversation with any woman. But you and I know each other. You've had a few rough patches in recent history. I'm not sure you should be jumping into a relationship. And don't act like you were remotely interested in starting anything with anyone. All you've talked about lately is this entertainment business and Tonea. You've been tight-lipped about your romantic life."

"And in case I forgot, you are here to remind me." Laxmi couldn't feel disappointed with Fiona's reasoning. After all, she had had the same talk with herself. Yet hearing it from Fiona did stiffen her back with muted outrage and a cold douse of shame. "You're right. I have no intention of having a relationship."

"Good. Besides, I have a few male friends who would be fun dates for you." Fiona's victorious smile broke through. "So you dropped him off at his hotel. Did he say if he had fun? Was he offended by anyone? I thought that I was playing it cool. Then when he left and I saw Grace's face, I turned into a fussy hen with her chick.

"Call me blindly optimistic, but I know that if we can get past the barrier in his mind, he'll see that we have good intentions. And you know my mother, who doesn't show much emotion, was so nervous around him. Caught her looking at him with quiet satisfaction. She's impressed with the man he's become. It still makes me a little misty."

Sure enough, Laxmi saw the tears glistening in Fiona's eyes. And she didn't know how to respond or what to do. Their mending friendship felt dangerously close to unraveling.

Laxmi texted Tonea out of desperation to slow the downward spiral of the mood. Where are you?

Based on how close Tonea was to the studio, she'd table this conversation with Fiona for another time. Her client was due to arrive at any minute. Time at the recording studio had been squeezed in between two interviews with local TV stations. While any further revelations would erupt under Fiona's protective attitude, Laxmi didn't want to hide anything about her and Dresden from her friend.

Tonea finally responded.

Sorry, got held up at the last interview. Traffic is horrible.

Go straight to the other interview, Laxmi texted back. We don't want to miss that one. See you there.

"You know, Fiona," Laxmi began, picking her words carefully, "you're stressing yourself out unnecessarily. You want this happy ending for your mom and Dresden so badly that you're kind of obsessing about it. A little too much, if you ask me."

"I'm the scary lady?"

"Kinda." Laxmi scrunched her face. "A lot of this is out of your hands. Feelings, reactions, motivation shouldn't be controlled or manipulated to suit our wishes."

"I want to talk to him. Face-to-face. Just so he knows where I'm coming from."

"That sounds good," Laxmi said encouragingly.

"I'm sorry that I jumped down your throat." Fiona offered her hand. "Sorry."

"You might not want to offer me a handshake."

"Oh?" Fiona's hand lowered, with the smile that slid away.

"In keeping with honesty at the expense of your anger, I didn't take Dresden to my hotel. I took him to his. And stayed."

"The night?"

"Hours." Laxmi's face heated, but not over sexy images of Dresden. The tension had exploded to fill every nook and cranny in the room. Fiona looked about to blow.

"Hours." Fiona repeated the word as if each utterance provided further clarity that turned to horror. "You didn't."

Laxmi nodded.

"How could you? Just like that? Who does that?"

"Does what? Enjoy a nice evening with someone they are attracted to? It's not that uncommon."

"But you don't know him. Nothing about him. Except after finding out he's a Meadows." Fiona's anger lifted off and swirled in fury.

"You're right. I heard 'Meadows' and saw an ATM machine. So, I lassoed him and made him pay me along with a little bump and grind." Laxmi underscored her sarcasm with an exaggerated wink. Her skin prickled with the heat of her indignation. "Now I'm paid and satisfied." She'd never indulged in one-night stands, even with the lousy guys that she'd attached herself to. It took a special man, on one hand, and her steps to be emotionally independent, on the other hand, to go with whatever felt right that night. Maybe she'd failed in that effort, too, because she hadn't, or couldn't, walk away as she'd hoped.

"You're being ridiculous."

"And you aren't. Don't tell me you weren't ready to jump all over your handsome Leo when you first saw him. The Meadows princess with the baby intern." Laxmi snorted. "Give me a break with the hypocrisy."

"I was young."

"I'm not dead. And for the record, I don't go around hopping into beds. Anymore."

"Except this happened." Fiona clapped her hands to her ears. "I don't want to hear any more."

"Okay, I won't tell you the details about my back against the wall." Laxmi enjoyed torturing her.

"If you don't stop talking, I'm going to tape your mouth."

"We would have tried tape, but we didn't have any."

"Why do I like you?"

Laxmi sighed. "We're alike but yet so different. And that's a good thing." She reached out and held on to Fiona's hand. "Look, if it makes you feel any better, it was a one-night thing. We both went into it with that mind-set. And we were cool with it." Laxmi avoided any disclosure on the ending scene that had taunted her to toss out her resolution and rejoin Dresden for an encore.

"I'm sorry that I turned into Miss Evil." Fiona sighed heavily.

"Never. We were BFFs. I know this is important. I plan to make it up to you," Laxmi blurted without having a clue what she could do to get on Fiona's good side. But she valued Fiona's friendship and acknowledged her own messy contribution to the situation.

"You're still my best friend. Through thick and thin."

They hugged, wiped a few stray tears away and laughed at their current state, relieved that they could move on together.

Laxmi didn't know how she would make up for lost time, but she knew it would mean reopening that door to go after Dresden all the way to Toronto. The mission to mend fences between Dresden and the Meadowses could prove difficult to help with while she kept a safe distance from any emotional entanglement with him. No matter the fallout, like her professional career, she had something to prove—but now it was to Fiona, that she was worthy of being her friend. She'd do her best to fulfill Fiona's wish for a reunion between Dresden and Verona, even if it meant spending time with a man she liked.

Chapter 5

Dresden studied the diverse faces looking back at him in the classroom. Mostly interested. Several, however, hadn't looked up from their laptops or phones to pay attention to the lecture. He always had to provide the right incentive to get his university students properly motivated. Since Grace's birthday party three weeks ago, his academic life at University of Toronto had settled back to normal.

"Do you have any questions so far?" he asked as he sometimes did throughout his presentations on the colonization of the Americas. He wasn't one to encourage students to hold their questions to the end. The back-and-forth added a great sidebar to his talks and lifted the energy within the group.

A disjointed wave of students shook their heads. Mainly blank stares responded to his inquiry. Again, he knew the solution for nonengagement.

"Okay. We'll move on to the next chapter."

Dresden launched into military and economic contributions of eighteenth-century black Canadians. He mentioned, among others, Richard Pierpoint, who had petitioned the government to protect the Niagara frontier; Josiah Henson, an escaped slave from Kentucky who helped others acclimate to freedom after their escape to Canada; and Mary Ann Shadd Cary, who came to Canada by way of the Underground Railroad and became the first female African American newspaper editor, along with teaching young children of former slaves. "And FYI, this information will be included on the final exam."

The dire promise spurred the room into action. Finally he had 100 percent participation—or more like 98. There were always one or two stubborn ones who had to learn the hard way not to ignore his content advisories about tests.

He dimmed the lights and rolled through another ten PowerPoint slides. With two minutes to spare, he reiterated the homework and upcoming assignments. As soon as the class ended, the students erupted out of the seats and created a bottleneck at the door.

One lone person in the audience remained—Laxmi.

Laxmi could listen to Dresden all day. His topic was interesting. But really, he was just gorgeous to look at, with a smooth, deep voice to heighten her desire. She doodled on a sheet of paper to give her gaze something else to focus on rather than feed her brain with images for her fantasies.

But now everyone had left, she'd have to face the consequences of her behavior after they'd made love. That was if he would give her the chance. She'd taken the bold step to arrive in Toronto and plead her case, if necessary, in person.

Not that she was confident that she could change his mind, but he deserved to know that her rejection wasn't about him. The knots of doubt now churning and multiplying had been there long before he arrived to wake her up.

She wanted one more chance to get it right.

Dresden squinted to double-check the truth of what he saw rather than rely on a romantic delusion that meant he needed bed rest.

"Popped in for a quick visit." She waved at him from an end seat on the last row.

"How long have you been in here?" He stayed behind the podium. His hands curled around the edges to anchor his excitement. His pulse ticked up.

Suddenly he was a nervous ten-year-old boy standing in front of class in a new school and talking about what he'd done over the summer. Spending time in the Sahara Desert with his parents on their latest assignment automatically excluded him from the excited chatter about beach trips or Disney park visits. His description of playing tag, or *sellenduq*, where one person pretended to be a jackal to tag others, with the nomadic Tuareg children, had produced the worst sort of hilarity and cruel comments from his new classmates. Like those days, he pushed the nerves aside, bit down on the unfairness and stayed put, not giving in to their behavior. He'd learned the tough way to appear neutral. He waited for Laxmi's response.

"I snuck in when it was dark. Your back was turned," she explained with a visible dose of pride.

Dresden gathered his papers and stuffed them in his

bag. There had been no expectation that he'd see her again. Her hurried departure had told him enough. She wasn't interested.

I'll let you go...for now.

His parting words to her still haunted him at the most inopportune times, such as when he should concentrate on driving, studying or teaching. Laxmi strutted into his thoughts like she did at the party's bar, undaunted by his unapproachable demeanor.

Despite his bold, cocky statement then, he still hadn't had a clue how to draw her back to him. She'd resisted all his pleas at the hotel and hadn't shown any signs that she'd wanted to be with him beyond that night. A stinging punch to the ego. But he'd managed to swallow the hurt while balancing a small nugget of hope like a lit candle at the window that she'd contact him.

When it looked as if she wouldn't change her mind after their impromptu meet-up, he'd dialed her number and had stopped just before pushing the button to engage the call. Beyond that certain wildness to her that excited him, he might be unable to hold her interest in the long term? His analytical side wanted to push for that vote.

The other part of him that rebelled against the comfortable reliance on order and routine couldn't stop the desire to be around Laxmi, to learn more about her and to do his best to seduce her.

Despite his inner turmoil, he timed his attempts to ask about her with any opportunities that popped up. The few times that he'd spoken to Fiona, he'd casually asked about everyone, including Laxmi. One time she'd followed up, probing about his interest in Laxmi, and he'd quickly backed off and redirected her attention. He wanted to keep the two worlds separated.

Laxmi was a gift from that night at Grace's party.

Though they'd barely touched on a personal subject, he wasn't ready to share or hear her perspective.

Opening up about the Meadowses was a bit like peeling off a bandage from his leg, removing one hair strand at a time. Even thinking about the family for a tiny bit could dampen his mood. When he was with Laxmi, the contemplation about his life with the stampeding Meadowses stayed pleasantly dormant.

But the minute that his mind pressed for deliberation, for an analysis, maybe closure, the Meadowses took over. With Grace's letter, he was the bystander told to join in at the tail end of the drama. With his parents' encouragement, he was to be gracious and magnanimous toward strangers.

Expectations of him were high. Too high.

And when it came to Fiona and the Meadowses, he'd stay on neutral land as much as possible and if possible. He'd use the same rule to keep things drama-free, when it came to Fiona and her best friend. Until he could deal with her family, he didn't want Fiona traipsing through his private business.

He looked up as Laxmi strutted toward him like a Hollywood siren. Stuffing papers into his briefcase was momentarily forgotten. He wasn't ready. The urge to bolt for the nearest exit designated for the teaching staff offered up a weak option. He stood still mesmerized as she took her time to join him.

"It was a pretty interesting discussion," she said. Her gaze looked over everything, including him, as if she had to study him up close. She fluffed her hair, which bounced and landed in a dark, curly mass past her shoulders.

He was sure her smile was an attempt to brush aside his doubts about why she hadn't called him, as if all his uncertainties were not grounded in facts. Cheery and assertive, her attitude didn't betray any misgivings on her part. She now breezed into his life without a concern, ready to pick up from their last hookup.

"I like teaching this class," he answered.

"I didn't like history classes when I attended college. Didn't appreciate the context and lessons to be learned from the past. Now that I'm older, I accept a little too late its dual role as entertainment and as life lessons."

"Yeah, and it has a way of keeping us accountable as we currently make our history." Dresden often encouraged students to use his lessons as a backdrop for talking about current events, for people to see how far society had come or as cautionary tales on how to proceed. But if he did only listen to his past, he'd give Laxmi a wide berth.

He held open the door for her and they walked side by side to his office. To fill any empty space, he pointed out architectural features of the university, the historical significance behind sculptures and impressive busts that decorated the halls.

"Warning. My office is a bit cluttered." Dresden winced as he led the way into his private space.

"Wow." Laxmi stood in the room with her hand covering her mouth. Her already bright eyes looked bigger as she took in his overflowing shelves to the stacks of books on the floor to the papers that covered the surface of his desk.

"My house is very neat and tidy," he said to minimize her judgment.

"That's because everything that is paper-related in your life is in here. You are a fire hazard."

"I'm not the worst," he protested while moving a stack of papers to be graded from the only chair.

"Where do you meet with your students?"

"In the conference room down the hall."

"I'm sure you've lost a freshman or two in here." She walked over to his bookshelf and read aloud the titles. "Although, from your private stash, I'd say you're pretty smart."

"All freshmen are accounted for. And I can do a lot of things, even nonacademic ones, at exceptional status. As you might know firsthand."

"Hmm." She turned her head, but not before he spied her lips lifting into a smile.

"Not that I don't like the impromptu visit, but what brought you to Toronto?"

"Actually, business. My client has gigs at a couple small venues, and since she's in upstate New York this week, I figured why not hop across the border, see Canada?"

"Good strategy." He gestured to the Keurig coffee machine. She nodded and pointed to the caramel-flavored pod. Once the machine started, he returned his attention to her. "Why the impromptu visit here? To my classroom?"

"Wanted to see you. In your world." She shrugged and tossed out a toothy smile. "I got curious."

"Took you long enough." He didn't want to sound petulant, but he'd been craving this woman and her ice-queen demeanor like an addict needing a fix. Now she'd tossed a crumb that curiosity in her busy schedule had delivered her to him.

The machine beeped its readiness.

"Your coffee." He handed her a mug and offered cream and sugar packs for her to doctor the piping-hot liquid.

"Thanks." She took a dainty sip and then licked her lips.

Why did the smallest movement from her produce

such big reactions from his body? He slid into his chair behind the desk. His senses short-circuited around her. In the small room, smelling so darn good, he couldn't function as Professor Haynes. He could easily become the stranger who'd enjoyed a one-night stand in a hotel room.

Their previous major interaction had been minimally verbal. Arms locked. Chest pressed against breasts. Legs around hips. Damn, his neck got hot in a quick second.

She reached into her purse and pulled out a small wrapped box. "I came bearing gifts. A peace offering of sorts."

He watched her slide the box to him on a paper that he'd used for his grocery list. "Should I shake it?"

"Go ahead."

He didn't; instead he unwrapped the box. The guesses of what it could be piled up in his head. Glances over the desk to Laxmi revealed nothing. She blinked at him with those long lashes and offered her tiny Mona Lisa smile.

The box. Focus.

The box. Keep his mind on the box. Don't look at her eyes. Her lips. *Please keep that tongue out of sight.*

"It's food?" He sniffed the item. Chocolate. A thick, circular treat. Still he wasn't sure what it was.

"Choco pies. Korean version of moon pies and my fave dessert on a snowy night."

Dresden held up the choco pie, flipping it from one side to the other for any hint of what lay beneath the choc-olate coating. "And this is a peace offering?"

"I would have made it, if I'd had the patience. Never been an expert in the kitchen." She motioned for him to eat. "It's quite delicious. But I planned ahead. If you didn't take me to your office, we would have gone to a café and shared the dessert. It's part of my diplomatic mission."

"Oh, really?" He held up the meaningful cake between them, but still only inspecting. What if he did play along?

"And it's bad manners to refuse."

"I have no intention of turning you down."

She blinked.

"Just wondered what took you so long." Dresden sipped his coffee and let his ego do the talking.

"I had to weigh the pros and cons."

"Hmm. So the pro column won? Yet you're in my office bribing with…this?"

"Gifting."

"*Gifting* me with unusual foods." He set the dessert on a napkin. "Then I will formally accept the gift." He tapped his coffee mug to hers and turned his attention on the chocolate pie.

"I don't know how you Canadians do it. But I seal delivery of my gifts with a kiss," she stated.

Dresden erupted in laughter. "Every time you say sorry, you kiss someone?" He refused to entertain that visual.

"I don't apologize often," Laxmi said with a jut of her chin. "And I don't go the extra mile on every apology."

"Never thought I was special…to you."

She leaned over and took the pie. Daintily she broke the circular treat in two. "Here." She fed him the chocolate-covered, thin-cake sandwich with marshmallow filling.

Dresden bit into the soft pie and thoughtfully chewed. After a few seconds of mulling over the sweet mixture, he nodded. "Different."

Before he could wipe the remnants off his lips, Laxmi leaned in and grabbed his shirt and pulled him toward her. She kissed him, sweeping his lips with hers, first with a softness that melted his spine and then with enough pressure to stoke his excitement and cause his willpower to completely collapse.

Before he lost consciousness, she let go and he sank back into the chair.

He felt aroused. Confused. Vulnerable.

"More?" she taunted.

"Nope." He pressed his back into his chair in case she sprang another trap for his emotions.

"We're not done with negotiations."

Dresden had a hard time getting his craving—his arousal—back to neutral. "Yeah, we're done."

Thanks to her flirtations, he was guaranteed another sleepless night, not only thinking about her but now their knee-buckling kiss. Did she have to return like a conquering queen to stir the dust and stake her flag?

"My gift didn't work." She looked thoroughly sad to the point that he wanted to reassure her. But this was Laxmi; the woman didn't hesitate to take control.

"It worked. We're talking," he offered.

"Well, I was hoping that after I kissed you, you would go hot, wild and sexy on the desk. You'd make a big sweep of all the papers while I'm in your arms. Pages would go flying everywhere like confetti as you rip open my blouse. Buttons would pop. With one hand you'd unsnap my bra and my breasts would spring free."

Dresden's laughter popped out at the visual of her breasts with their brown-tipped nipples *springing free*. Actually, what his imagination created and what he knew about the beauty of her body took his breath away.

"And then you'd kiss them." She pointed to her chest. "Here and here."

His eyes followed the tip of her index finger to the smooth fabric of her blouse. "You have a lot of expectations."

"I'm an optimist. You have to be to survive in this entertainment game."

He'd kept his piece of optimism alive the night she'd driven off and he'd been left wishing that she'd make a U-turn and pull up at the hotel's curb again.

Then he'd held out hope that she'd call him. How many times had he checked his voice mail? He'd looked at his emails coming up with lame excuses for her dismissal of him.

Optimism could go to the wayside. That word and sentiment never really fit his current lifestyle. Not with the Meadowses. Not with Laxmi.

"Good. I like a challenge." She leaned back and put her feet on the edge of his desk and crossed them. "I'm here for a couple of nights. So, if you're willing…"

"Another booty call?"

"If that's what you want to call it."

"Nah. I'll pass." His heart thudded like a sledgehammer against his chest. The tension between them was almost too much to bear. But his ego wasn't ready to give up the point position.

She set down the dessert. Clearly she hadn't expected that reaction. She stared for a few seconds into her cup.

"Need more coffee?" he continued.

She shook her head. "I thought you'd want to hook up. It worked well last time."

"Last time? Consider that a big fail." No more innuendos and witty metaphors. Time to have a heart-to-heart with this woman who tormented his sanity.

"Wasn't a fail from where I stood, especially with my back against the wall and my leg hitched around your hip."

Dresden's face warmed, but he forced the memory to take a back seat. He had to make his point. "We went in with mutual understanding. But once we opened up to each other, I had second thoughts. I wanted more. You, however, went into retreat behind a wall of indifference. How could I renegotiate the terms? Terms that were too restrictive."

He set down his cup and walked around the desk until he stood near her chair. Until she walked out of his office, he would stand his ground to make his point. "I know that I got to you. I know that a little bit of ice thawed and there was a shift. But you shut it down and shut me out without breaking a sweat."

Laxmi.

"I protected myself." She stared straight ahead, but he didn't allow that to stop him from sitting on the front edge of the desk to continue with his case.

"I wasn't a threat." His voice dropped, his tone low and steady. He hoped that nothing he'd done had rattled her confidence in him.

"No man gives me terms and conditions. My rules. My life."

The faraway look, the coldly distant declaration, spoke of a history he didn't know.

Instead of giving up, Dresden treaded carefully. "And those rules are never broken? Never revised?" His fingers ached to touch her, to comfort and hold her.

She put her cup down and looked up at him. "Why should they be? And who would make that happen?" Her eyebrows shot up as she issued the challenge.

Dresden crossed his arms and studied his visitor. The glint in Laxmi's eyes clued him in that she was thoroughly enjoying the sparring. But he wasn't foolish enough to think she didn't mean every word. He held his tongue to force her to continue talking.

"So let's get back to why I'm here. You're truly not

going to jump on the offer?" She crossed her legs and clasped her hands at her knees. Her grin was pure sin.

"The arrangement doesn't suit my terms, my conditions. And I have no intention of becoming your cabana boy for the occasional pelvic thrusts."

"Even if you know it would feel so damn good?" She rose out of the chair with such graceful ease that he was caught unaware.

Resting her hands on his thighs, she pressed her fingers into his flesh. Slowly she stroked his upper legs.

His crotch tightened and pulsed with every upward slide of her hands. His breath hissed. She was playing dirty. And winning.

"No strings mean no drama. An ideal situation, if you ask me." She bit her lip. Her head tilted at an angle primed for a kiss.

"No deal." His jaw clenched in a major fight to stop his body's traitorous lean to her side. "Since I don't have classes for the rest of the day, I want you in my house today, for three days, two nights. Nothing less." He tilted her chin so he could see her, look deep into her soul. And if she leaned a smidgen closer, he might even kiss her. That was, if he couldn't restrain himself.

"Now, why would I do that? I'm here on business." She stopped stroking his thighs and he almost begged her to continue.

"Not stopping you from conducting business. As a matter of fact, I'd love to see you do your thing."

Clearly she hadn't expected that request. Her mouth opened, but then, with a slight shake of her head, she closed it.

He resisted smoothing away the frown from her forehead. "You don't strike me as the type to walk in fear. You get what you want and I get what I want." The art of negotiation wasn't a strength he'd ever boasted. Besides, his prowess at fostering romantic relationships wasn't a thing. With Laxmi he was working on gut instinct.

"Still no strings," she persisted.

"Fine. It's one long one-night stand. Again." He'd call his victory whatever she wanted to name the momentous occasion. All he cared was that she would be on his turf for a blip in time, but enough for him to convince her they should have ongoing one-night stands.

"I need my phone." She pulled it out of her pocket-book.

He waited for her to share what she was about to do.

She walked away, but not far, considering the size and cluttered effects of his office.

What if she had plans with someone? He'd been too happy to see her return to consider the possibility.

She dialed then wedged the phone between her ear and shoulder as she rummaged through her bag. "I have to cancel my hotel room."

His relief whooshed out of his lungs. "I'll make it worth your while."

"Not remotely worried about that." She turned her attention to her call.

Dresden carried through with his pretense of nonchalance as he walked over to the only window in the room. With his back to her, he looked out on the campus oval where the other buildings circled the large green patch with its intersecting walk paths. Despite the particularly cold day, he felt cozy and warm with a good dose of nerves that he'd invited Laxmi into his life.

"I'm ready."

Dresden replied, "So am I."

Chapter 6

Dresden kept his phone within easy reach. Maybe he was the fool to believe that luck had swayed to his side. Doubts forced him to act like a lookout scout pining for any signs of Laxmi's arrival—monitoring his phone and looking down onto the streets of his condominium from the fifteenth floor. He paced like a nervous sentry.

Earlier, when he and Laxmi had left his office, she'd sent him on with a parting message that she'd see him later. Their recent coming together over a choco pie dictated that he shouldn't be worried she'd ditch him again. If so, then his grand plan to knock her off balance with his impromptu request had failed.

Despite all the sexy banter and innuendo, and despite the surprise negotiations, he didn't trust Laxmi to uphold her end. Why would she? She wasn't the one losing God's good sense to be with someone. Her exceptional ability to turn off her emotions proved she wasn't the one in a state of turmoil. Only time would undo the knots, a luxury he didn't have with her, but it was the point of his invitation for her to stay at his home. Find and take every chance to be with her and get closer each time.

But what did this ultimately mean for him? Or his actions? Pining after a woman wasn't his thing, nor was spending hours creating options A through Z to change her mind in his favor.

On a normal day his focus stacked his priorities around family, then teaching, writing, lectures and not much of anything else. Sharing his time with anyone never disrupted what was already established in his life. Usually his relationships were ways to pass time between projects. They were fluid. No one got tired of the other. No one rejected the other—a word that his parents insisted he never use to describe his adoption. Maybe more than the word had stuck with him. Maybe there was no way to disguise the reality.

With casual relationships, his attitude protected him. Placed him in the control seat. Most times his "girl-friends" were colleagues on scholarly visits who turned into temporary companions. The arrangements suited his lifestyle with its handy expiration dates.

During those times, the highlights of their discussions centered on the latest slants on an ancient philosophy, historical hypotheses, or kicking around possible dissertation questions for the latest round of candidates. From Sweden to Tanzania, from Tonga to Guyana, his colleagues shared great conversation and intimacy without raising his pulse. And when they'd return to their universities, fond memories momentarily lingered until he got busy with life.

Until the past year, he could make the claim that his life barely entertained any ripples to unbalance what was important to him. The phase of his life called the Meadows Invasion.

The revelation of his adoption wasn't a big deal. His parents had never hid the reality. By the time he'd started elementary school, they had taken the time to tell him amid tight hugs and sincere repetitions of "we love you." He had soaked up the news as good-to-know, but it hadn't and wouldn't change his life. Or so he'd thought.

Fate might as well have been a school-yard bully who took decisive pleasure in smashing into him with a left hook to his world and a right uppercut to his emotions. He was conflicted over the steady additions of the people in his life. And his emotional balance couldn't right itself on the tumultuous waves. Nothing he'd learned so far explained the why. Why had Verona given him away? Was it nothing more than her fear of being judged for her actions?

He didn't know he had the anger balled up in a giant knot residing in his heart. He didn't know that the anger had a target—Verona, his biological mother. And he didn't know that he had cared about being a secret while she'd happily moved on with family, all nice and proper for society's standards. From his point of view, he would much rather be only responsible for himself. And if he'd never received that letter from Grace, he'd be ignorant of how late her discovery of him had come.

But the part of him that survived, feeling like a stranger in the many far-flung places his traveling parents called home, or an outcast when they returned to Canada, had come up for air and never left. There was some fight in him.

The fighter withstood the Meadowses. Fiona, however, was the exception. Her sincerity and respect of his personal space counted a lot with him. But while she wanted more and hoped that he'd let in the rest of the family, he couldn't hand her that victory. He'd vowed that his relation to the Meadowses was in DNA only. Every other link from him to them had been erased.

On the other hand, running into Laxmi at the event he'd initially refused to attend was maybe fate's half-hearted apology. Or fate showed its wicked sense of humor over his whiny moping about a woman in a heart-melting red dress. For all the so-called fight in him, he was soft Play-Doh in Laxmi's hands…if she only knew.

From across the room, his phone pinged. He rushed for it—excitement already mounting. So much for playing it cool.

I'm here in lobby

OK. Be down in a sec

He grinned, a bit embarrassed with his sense of relief. Most of the doubts pulled up their stakes and skittered away into the shadows. The weight on his shoulders lightened.

On the way out, he sized up his appearance in the mirror. Nothing stuck in between the teeth. Hair had been recently shaped up. Maybe he should have changed out of the grandpa sweater. There was no time. Nerdy professor would have to be his fashion statement.

He lightly jogged down the hall to the elevator banks. His finger impatiently stabbed at the button until the doors opened. Nerves had him pacing in the car on its descent. By the time Dresden stepped onto the lobby floor, his pace was revved into a fast walk toward the hospitality area of his condo building.

"Good to see you." He briefly touched her arm.

"It's been a while," she teased.

"You look great."

"Same as three hours ago."

Dresden shook his head. "You changed your outfit."

"I call this my ninja gear."

With her coat hanging over her arm, she sported an all-black ensemble with a turtleneck that hugged her top half and modestly draped over her hips while leggings molded her bottom half. Silver jewelry decorated her ears and wrist, along with a pair of ankle-high black boots that completed the sexy attire.

"Ninja?" he asked.

"I can blend in and be agile. Just in case I have to disappear through the tiniest space in a solid wall and scale insurmountable heights."

"Your madcap dash to freedom won't be necessary. It's not a fortress. But I'm sure your agility will come in handy for other uses." As Dresden spoke, he realized she didn't have an overnight bag. Wasn't she staying? Was he supposed to go along with her pretense because she stood in his building joking about leaving?

"My hesitation isn't because of something you said or have done. It's not fear that had me driving down Yonge Street, making a loop three times around the building. I needed more time to think. Should I continue on with this game or head back to my hotel?"

"See, I would take offense to my invitation being called a game if I believed that you really thought it was." Dresden stepped into the elevator car and waved his key fob over the sensor before pushing the button for his floor. "Going up?"

She barely had time to slip her hand between the steadily closing doors to make them reopen. "You could have been a gentleman," she scolded as she entered.

"I was. You were free to avoid stepping on for the ride."

She pursed her mouth. The words, he was sure, roiling around in that pretty head were ready to scorch him. He winked to add to her aggravation.

Dresden led the way down the hallway. They passed a few of his neighbors returning home from their jobs or taking their dogs for an afternoon walk. The exchanges of greetings were pretty much the extent of any conversation. Meanwhile, Laxmi stayed quiet with lips pressed firmly together.

"Welcome." Dresden beckoned Laxmi into his condo. He took her coat, which for a second she stubbornly pinned between her forearm and body.

"Stop looking smug."

"I promise, I'm not." He crossed his heart, bracing himself for when she'd tell him that it was time for her to get back to the hotel. Despite their last passionate encounter, they had ended out of sync with each other. Now he remained tentative, trying to read the signs in advance.

"You're gloating."

"It's not a win or lose." He sighed. "It's never been a game."

"You mess with my head. And I don't like that." She wrapped her finger around a coil of her hair.

So, he wasn't the only one on a dizzy merry-go-round. Still, he kept that revelation to himself. He paused at the closet with her coat ready to be placed on a hanger.

"You may hang up my coat. I'm not leaving. And I'm here because I wouldn't want to be elsewhere."

He nodded and proceeded with the task. Hopefully he could muddle through their time together without sounding like a movie special. "I'll show you to your room."

"My suitcase is in my car."

"Oh, I thought you were planning to go au naturel for the weekend. And I'm down with a decision, if you wish." He raised a hand for a high five, which she rewarded with a slap-down from her hand.

"Had to check out the vibe of your place."

Dresden led the way from the foyer past his bedroom to the second room. He entered and looked around, hoping its decor would appeal to her.

She entered and stood next to him. In a slow 360-degree motion, her gaze swept over the area. He followed along, trying to see things as a new visitor, noting the walls painted in a hint of blue with soft white trimmings. The mirrored closet doors added depth to the space that was not expansive, hence the full-size bed with its duvet cover to match the walls.

"The bathroom has two doors—one is here in the room and the other opens into the hallway. My bedroom has its own bathroom, so no worries that you must share this with me," he joked, under pressure from a case of the nerves. He had to make light of the situation rather than face the tiny possibility of sharing such an intimate place with her.

"Very different from the office." She pulled out one of three James Patterson's Alex Cross detective books on a bookshelf. "Yep, very different vibes."

"Works for you?" He really wasn't worried. Her relaxed, playful manner had dissipated the earlier tension.

"Yes. You see, in your office, I wanted to go for it on your desk. To be cocooned by paper and books in the hallowed halls of academia and naked under you struck me as an ideal situation."

He gulped.

"In here, I like the soothing effect of the colors. And with the light pouring in from there, I wouldn't mind going traditional." She ran her hand across the width of the bed.

He cleared his throat. "Um… I'll let you get comfortable, while I get us a drink. Wine?"

"That's good. And I'll run down and get my bag." She plucked the key fob from his palm. "Be right back."

He stepped back for her to pass and didn't move until he heard the door softly close. If he continued holding his breath every time she was inches from him, he was likely to pass out. But he hoped by the end of her visit they would be comfortable with each other, nestled against each other's bodies, without planning to hightail it out of each other's lives.

Dresden headed to the kitchen and pulled out a chilled bottle of Riesling, popped the cork and poured two generous portions of the wine. On a small plate, he arranged a few crackers and cheese squares. Should he put on music? If so, then what was her taste? Or was that going too far down the nerd route? But with his grandpa sweater, he definitely wouldn't be mistaken for Don Juan.

Laxmi headed to her car for her small suitcase. She needed this short space of time to accept the realization that she was back with Dresden, even staying with him. She grinned at passersby, happily sharing her giddy feelings.

Considering how much she'd hid from the public and how beat down she'd felt, this new turn in her life felt like a release from an emotional prison. One that she'd built around herself.

Although Fiona wouldn't understand what she'd endured and what she now felt, she had to believe that she was heading in the right direction.

Dresden's strength and solid footing were attractive.

But there was a strong sense of empathy of what he might be feeling toward the Meadowses. And she didn't mind coaxing him along not only for Fiona's sake, but also for his own sake.

The front door opened and he popped his head out of the kitchen.

"I'm back." She dropped his key on the dining table and headed down the hall to the bedroom.

"Let me know if there's anything you need."

"Will do. Besides, I don't have much to put away."

"When you're done, I've got a glass of wine and some nibbles before we head out to dinner."

She didn't respond and he presumed she was busy in the bedroom.

Feeling relieved and satisfied with the outcome so far, he set down the wineglasses, along with the plate of food, before he settled on the couch to wait for her. He stretched his arms out along the back of the couch and crossed his legs propped on the table. Who knew the day would have turned out to be a fantastic one?

"Looks like you're already relaxed and ready for the weekend." She joined him on the couch. He noticed her shoes were gone, as she sat cross-legged next to him.

"Your wine." He handed her the glass.

"Thanks." She sipped and smacked her lips. "Delicious."

He offered the plate and waited for her to stack the cheese onto a cracker. "What do you feel like eating for dinner? We can head out or have it delivered."

"I can't." She made a face. "Tonea has a gig tonight."

"Oh." He understood that she really hadn't come to Toronto for his sake. "I'll keep the porch light burning for you," he joked.

"Why don't you come with me? We can grab something to eat at the bar."

"People and loud music—what's not to love?" Dresden clinked glasses with her. "To Tonea."

"To living life to the fullest," she added, the perfect sentiment to the evening.

They sipped wine and descended into a noisy game of tossing the square cheese into each other's mouths.

"Your aim is lousy," he accused as the cheese hit his forehead and disappeared over the couch.

"Your mouth isn't big enough."

Dresden picked up a cheese square from the plate, squinted an eye before taking aim and tossed it directly into her mouth. "I'm so damned good, I need to get an award for your crushing defeat."

"If I win, I'll cook breakfast."

"And if you win, I'll… Oh, heck, that ain't gonna happen." His teasing earned him two cheese squares ricocheting off his cheeks.

With the food either eaten or littering his living room, the space on the couch narrowed between them. Her legs were crossed on top of Dresden's. His hands casually draped over her legs.

"I pictured you as a happy chef in your kitchen."

He looked for signs of her teasing, but she wore a serious expression. "I'm more of a foodie. Lived too many places and got to enjoy lots of meals that I couldn't replicate. So why waste time in the kitchen fumbling around when I can speed-dial a dish of pad thai or Bulgogi?"

"Sounds like you didn't have any reason to hone your cooking skills. I aim to fix that while I'm here, for my benefit, of course."

He snorted but sobered at her withering glance. "Fine. Pick what meal it will be."

"Why do you think it will be one meal? We'll start at the beginning of the day and work our way down to a decadent dessert by the evening."

"Okay. My contribution is eggs and toast." He added his touch to her grand plans.

"No thanks to the most boring breakfast ever, no way. I want *Barefoot Contessa*–type food. She fills her entire tabletop with massive spreads, a feast fit for a village."

"Who?" He didn't relish having to look up recipes on the internet. Besides, he already had the bread and eggs.

"Never mind. Just make sure to satisfy my hunger. It's been a while since I've taken the time to eat."

"And what time do you rise?" Now that he had his assignment, he looked forward to trying to wow her.

"Doesn't matter. Whenever you're done, just set it down. The smell of bacon can also work wonders with waking me up."

"You sure are specific. What do you normally eat for breakfast?"

"Three cups of coffee."

"Whoa. Sounds like your time with me will be a rehab on your digestive system. I look forward to the challenge."

"You think that you can change me with the snap of your fingers? I'm a tough bird."

"Stubborn is more like it, but that's your charm." He cupped her feet, a move that startled her, but she emitted a grateful moan as he gently massaged her feet and lower legs. Her muscles relaxed as he worked away the tension.

"It has to be breakfast in bed. Another treat that has eluded me," she moaned in pleasure.

"Because you don't stick around for the sunrise." He didn't judge, considering his own baggage.

"Means you are the lucky one. I'll be here."

"So you'll push pause on the ninja mission?"

"Feed me and I'll let you know." She pointed her toe and poked at his rib cage.

Dresden pulled her toward him. "I will feed you. I will satisfy you. And I will have you begging for more."

"Promise."

"A guarantee."

She stretched under his hand, which roamed all over her body but avoided the swell of her breasts and the valley between her legs.

Her back arched. "Stop teasing and touch me."

"Wouldn't dream of teasing." He winked and slid her legs off his. "Warming you up to face the cold night air, that's all. Anyway, we need to get ready, don't you think?"

"So it's going to be like that. You winding me up and leaving me to solo it on the way back down." She eyed him crossly.

"That would sound like I had a plan. That I was being manipulative. That I didn't care about your feelings." He tossed back the rest of his wine and finished with a loud *ah*. "The only thing that is a guarantee is my hospitality for the next three days. I'm going with the mood as my guide for anything else—turning it on, turning it off. Or just letting it simmer. Isn't that your motto?"

She stood and smiled in a manner that warned him to be wary. "The difference here is that I'm good at living up to my motto. Remember? My life. My rules." She walked out of the room before he could muster a witty reply.

Dresden blew out a breath. He rubbed his eyes hard with the heels of his hands. Maybe his ego had gone too far to make him think he could act unaffected for several days. This alpha-male stuff was hard work.

Chapter 7

Maybe inviting Dresden to come along for Tonea's first live performance in upstate New York wasn't a good idea. He was serenity on steroids, while Laxmi would have gnawed on her nails if it wasn't for her recent manicure. The crowd, or lack of one, usually set the dial for her nerves on frazzled. This time, Dresden was single-handedly the only one with the power to be in control.

She reluctantly admitted that not only did his presence screw with her balance but his opinion mattered. While she didn't worry about being judged elsewhere, like in the bedroom, she cared about what he thought of her as a businesswoman. Seeing a glimpse of his professional side made her wonder how he'd analyze her skills. How would he grade her? Could she pass muster?

Too many articles had marked her fast rise and epic fall to the bottom. Their candid, sometimes downright mean, judgments matched her own self-assessment, but hurt nonetheless. Now that she had turned the corner to climb back up the mountain, she didn't want the stench of her failures to cling to her or her artist. If it meant pretending that she had her wits about her and her business plans were sound, then she'd continue with the job.

As a result, the pressure for success mounted on her shoulders. She had much to prove, and splitting attention between Dresden and her business better not nudge her off track.

She looked at him and soaked up his bright smile with a little trepidation. If only she had the power to freeze this momentum in time with Dresden.

Was he a pleasurable distraction? Or was he a necessity to her life that would uplift her and help her succeed?

And she knew the answer she'd give if pushed. Her track record for relying on a man to inspire her was pathetic. So why torture herself by desiring anything beyond a fling?

Lights dimmed and the stage lights lit the microphone area where Tonea would stand. The emcee introduced her to a hearty round of applause. A good sign. Laxmi silently thanked the small group for the kindness showed to her newbie.

One problem. Tonea didn't step out to the stage.

Laxmi swore under her breath. *Come on, Tonea. You can do this.*

"Were you able to encourage her?" Dresden slid onto the bar stool next to Laxmi's. His hand offered up a cold bottle of beer.

She took the gift, but set it down. "I think I did. Gosh, I hope I did. It's our ritual for her to freak out and for me to hold her hand and calm her nerves. One of the main reasons I've booked these small venues."

"Good thinking."

"Should help to build her confidence and teach her how to work a room."

"Is that what you did?"

"Only for the first year. I was too hungry and too impatient to put in the time at the beginning to build loyal fans. Had a lot to prove." She stopped talking, uncomfortable with sharing too much about her failed dream. What powered her daily drive to succeed would stay hidden within her heart.

Laxmi offered up a quick prayer: *Please don't let her stage fright stop the show.*

"She was okay when you left her, right?" Dresden's concern joined with hers.

"Yes. When I left her this evening, she had the usual nerves, but she seemed cool." Laxmi slid off the bar stool to check on her. The show would begin in a few minutes with Tonea stepping onstage to wow another impressed crowd and adding more to her loyal fan base.

The roar of the crowd stopped her as Tonea finally emerged with a big smile and cheery wave to the audience. The stylist's recommendation for the young woman—a simply designed white dress with a bodice dusted lightly with silver sequins—was on point. Her hair was braided and wound into a crown that added an impression of soft elegance. Her makeup had a more theatrical look with her eyes shimmering with frosted shadow and defined liner. The effect transformed her, giving her an angelic persona as she belted out the first soulful note of her recent single.

Laxmi relaxed, somewhat. Her little diva would be all right.

"She's darn good." Dresden had joined in with the crowd to sing the catchy, easy-to-remember chorus.

Laxmi had to admit that she was proud. The hard work had paid off. She hoped the confidence would kick in so that it wasn't going to be a lengthy process to get Tonea onstage at each gig. No sense in her and her client feeling on edge.

As a manager, she had her hands ready to give Tonea a gentle push through obstacles or to catch her when she stumbled. She wouldn't let the business devour the young woman, to harden her heart and turn her against her dream. Laxmi had to be the bodyguard on that front.

"You would never guess that she'd had any problems." Dresden's animated support was a funny sight as he hollered "Tonea" in a booming voice. He paused in his exuberant yells to lean close to Laxmi's ear. "I'm convincing everyone that she's got the 'it' factor."

"Or you are the old guy who doesn't get out much." Laxmi giggled at Dresden's next antic when he joined hands with nearby patrons and swayed to the melody.

She remained on the bar stool, enjoying it all.

Before long, she was clapping along to the beat. From the look of things, Tonea was soaking up the adulation. A glow lit up her entire body, adding an energy that lifted her to a higher realm. Laxmi left her place at the bar to join in with the overhead wave, rocking in time with the rest of the audience and Tonea.

Laxmi hadn't been this mellow in a long time. Rebuilding her reputation, even among her friends, pushed her to walk a hard road at times. When important pieces of her life didn't fit neatly together like a jigsaw puzzle, she wished she could rely on good luck to make it all better. Not that she shouldn't deserve a bit of happiness, but after a drought of anything going right in her life, this unexpected break in the clouds refreshed her.

Once the song ended, she resumed her seat and sipped on her beer. Contentment settled in and allowed her to enjoy the rest of the show. Dresden looked over at her with the widest grin and plucked her beer out of her hand. He took a quick swig and returned it to her, adding a quick wink before he cheered at the end of another song. The casual, yet intimate, gesture felt good.

Laxmi gulped down a mouthful of beer to quell the heated eruptions of desire when he did things like wink.

He winked. She wanted him.

He smiled. She wanted him.

He laughed. And, all day and night, she wanted him.

Bottom line, she was losing all control over the lock on her heart. He came with his own special decoder ring that magically gained access and pushed open the doors to her life.

A full reveal scared her, however. Granted, she judged her own life through a harsh lens, but her career had set her up to be analyzed and reviewed. That road didn't always have the most scenic of views. No way could she trust Dresden with the potholes and patchwork of corrections to her mistakes. Shame wielded its power to keep her in check.

The solution didn't require deep thought. Keep Dresden within arm's reach, but with the emotional distance to survive his charm. She expected their battles of wills to continue for the sole purpose that she couldn't lose control and fall hard for him. That was way too easy to do.

As if he sensed her uneasiness, Dresden looked over at her. He cupped her cheek and stroked her face. "Don't worry. You've got a special lady up there. You believe in her. I believe in you. Congratulations, Madame Manager."

"Thanks." She wanted to whimper under his touch.

When he offered his hand, she hesitated for a second. She needed to know that she still could resist, if only for a smidgen of time. His hand closed around hers and their fingers interlocked between their bar stools. Her body sank into his with her arm pressed against his. Gosh, she was weak. Her willpower had slid off the stool to the floor, where it lay spineless.

Laxmi did her best to relax and enjoy the remainder of Tonea's performance and two encores. From the back, where she preferred to sit for Tonea's concerts, she assessed the crowd. She scanned the audience's participation and connection to the singer's energy.

In the beginning Tonea had tended to perform her songs as if just the first few rows were there. They'd worked on projection and thinking about individual people sitting in the seats or standing, instead of seeing the rest of the room as faceless darkness without a pulse. Her mental notes on the performance would be discussion points tomorrow.

Low-energy performances killed reputations, especially on social media, where frustrated fans had no problem dishing out harsh criticism. Early on, Tonea had learned that lesson.

"I'll be right back." She hated having to let go of Dresden's hand, but she was at work. And the celebratory atmosphere, although enjoyable, didn't diminish the tedious parts of her multiple roles as agent, manager, personal assistant and therapist.

"Go do your stuff—I'll be right here." Dresden shooed her away with a soft pat on her backside.

She nodded and turned to tackle the shifting wall of bodies. Squeezing through the crowd wasn't going to be easy. Oh, well, sitting in the back of the room had its drawbacks.

"Come on. I got you." Dresden walked up and overtook her. His shoulders squared and he effortlessly parted a path for them.

She held on to his waist because he *encouraged* people to step aside, his wide shoulders and strong arms cutting a path. The patrons stayed apart long enough for Laxmi to follow.

The muscular span of his back shielded hers as they wound their way like a snake through the reeds. This close, she wanted to rest the side of her face against his muscled back. Finally, they reached the end where patrons didn't cross the line to go backstage. Dresden opted to stay put now that his escort service was no longer needed.

Laxmi entered the backstage area after showing badges. At the same time, Tonea took her last bow and exited after kissing both hands and blowing them to the screaming fans. Laxmi smiled as Tonea basked in the adulation. But once the young woman spied Laxmi, she ran toward her manager with outstretched arms.

"Hey, doll, you had the room by that first note." Laxmi hugged her tightly.

"I was so nervous." Tonea grinned. The performance afterglow lit her face. Her eyes danced in time with her giddy mood. "I was afraid that I'd forget my lyrics. But I didn't. Could you tell when I did mess up?"

Laxmi shook her head. "You're fine. You looked fantastic."

"I think trying the meditation helped."

"Keep working on your meditation exercises so that when you have your gigs, you could do them anywhere. Having that calm, clear mind takes practice."

Tonea nodded. She patted the moisture off her face and neck.

"Okay, let me tie up any loose business ends and I will take you to the hotel. I'm sure you'll want to kick back and relax."

"This hairpiece will be the first thing off my head.

And you do not have to take me next door. I'm quite capable of crossing the street and walking into the hotel." Tonea shook her head at Laxmi's protests. "You're like a mother hen. Anyway, I'll see you in the morning?"

"Of course. We have the interview with the newspaper and then with the community TV station."

"Hopefully they are decent. Sometimes those questions about my personal life are a bit much."

"Yeah, not sure why they head down that route. It's no one's business who you're dating. But don't ever feel you must give an answer. Be polite, but firm, and you'll set the tone for your interviews."

"Okay. I'll try to summon my inner Laxmi. She's hidden deep under all my fears and insecurities." Tonea laughed.

"Heck, I might need to borrow her for myself. She might be on a long vacation." They laughed as they walked to the tiny dressing room that held Tonea's suitcase of makeup and clothes. "Since I'm not taking you back to your hotel, I'll go chat with the manager now."

Laxmi wanted the venue manager to remember Tonea. With a summer tour with other artists or as an opening act for an established artist, they could give the year a power surge with additional appearances to break through the saturated field of hungry artists. Tonea's desire and stamina would be tested. Two areas that had murky enough conditions to worry Laxmi.

"Your girl was a hit." The manager hurried past Laxmi with only a glance and nod of his head.

"I think so, too." She changed direction and kept pace with him. "Would love to do some repeat business."

"Good. I like to hear that artists had a good time." He poked his head out the emergency door and yelled at his staff huddled in the cold, smoking and chatting. "Give my booking agent a call. See what's on the calendar. She's a good kid. I wish her well."

Laxmi could tell there wouldn't be much more to the conversation as he hurried off to bark more orders. But she'd gotten what she'd needed to proceed ahead.

Tonea and Dresden were laughing together. He looked up as if sensing when she'd walked into the room and waved.

"Introductions already done?" Laxmi asked as Dresden helped her on with her coat.

"Yeah, Professor Haynes has been holding class."

"Professor Haynes, is it?" Laxmi had a hard time picturing him in his scholarly role. Too many sexy thoughts— unless he was a sexy introverted professor and she played the devilish student bent on taking him down with all sorts of carnal pleasures. She giggled.

She cleared her throat and tried to pull herself together. Her cheeks took a minute to cool. Her body's desire didn't budge.

"Actually, I was dropping some knowledge." His eyes narrowed. A small smirk played on his lips, letting her know he suspected the nature of her thoughts.

"The importance of an education," Tonea clarified.

"Are you trying to talk my client out of her dream?" She poked him in his firm abs. Tonea had had that argument with her parents before she'd opted to give her music 100 percent focus.

"Not hardly." Dresden clasped her hand between his.

If he only knew what his touch did to her.

"Professor Haynes says education enhances your dream. That you never stop learning about whatever it is that you want to do or achieve."

Tonea clearly had become his apt student.

"Good advice. Basically, life is one long lesson that

presents you with success and failures as part of the learning process." Laxmi added her insight.

"I'll deal with all of that after my year is up." Tonea scrunched her face.

"Year?" Dresden asked.

Laxmi looked at Tonea for a sign that she could share the deal made with her parents. The young woman offered a slight nod. "She has a year to prove that her dream is worthy. If not, she has to enroll in college."

"Ah…well, I think that's a smart plan. Don't dwell on 'if you don't make it.' You've got a plan, a great manager, so focus on the present. And do your best."

"Thank you." Tonea beamed. Her eyes looked a little misty. "Well, you go on ahead. I'm fine to get back. I'll even text you." She walked behind them and pushed them toward the door.

"Nope. When I'm around, I'll always make sure you get home or to the hotel." Laxmi looked up at Dresden. "Ready? Let's get out of here. I've got a long day ahead of us." She shared Tonea's schedule with Dresden.

"Sounds like breakfast plans are on hold," he whispered in Laxmi's ear as they headed out.

She shook her head. "You're not getting off that easily."

"You're quiet," he remarked as he navigated the final turn into his building's underground garage. "Tired?"

"Nope." She smothered a yawn. "Not fair with the power of suggestion. You made me do that."

"Don't blame me. I'm sure it's been a long day for you. And that you've been up pretty darn early."

She couldn't deny anything. But although she should be tired, sitting beside Dresden and thinking about the night ahead of her brushed the sleepiness aside.

They chatted and laughed all the way into the condo.

Laxmi headed to the room to get into more comfortable clothing. In an oversize T-shirt, minus the bra, and lounge pants, she joined Dresden in the living room. He'd also changed into sweats.

"Wine?" He held up the remainder of the Riesling.

"Nah. Need to keep the brain clear for tomorrow's activities."

"Will you have time for a mini tour of Toronto?"

"I'd love to, but I'd better play it by ear. Although we have the schedule, I've learned not to be tied to it. My priority doesn't mean it's the same for the interviewer."

"Plus, I kinda inserted me in there." He patted the seat next to him on the couch.

She didn't move. "And I don't want an apology. But I'm not sorry." Although she acknowledged the invite with a nod. "I'd rather do something else." Her finger wrapped around the hem of her T-shirt. She eased it up to offer a peep show of her abs. His gaze lowered but resumed its original position directly on her face.

His stoic expression almost cooled her enthusiasm. But ever so slightly, his nostrils flared. His Adam's apple bobbed and bobbed again. And there was no way she would have missed the bulge of his arousal.

She grinned. "Professor Haynes, could we go over what I need to do for extra credit?"

Chapter 8

Her bare feet didn't make a sound against the heated floor. Slowly she walked toward him. Nothing premeditated guided her actions. Something took hold of her—wild and free.

Laxmi knelt on the couch and straddled Dresden's thighs. Drowning in the depths of his dark eyes suited her. Her heartbeat thudded against her chest. Why was she a basket of nerves when this was what she wanted?

Because he excited her, drawing on all her senses in a heady mix where she lay in his arms. In other ways he soothed her anxieties with his orderly way of life.

His hands slid up her thighs and targeted her hips, where they rested. She looked down at them, hoping he wouldn't remove them from her body. It felt too good to go without the pleasure.

"You know you can't watch TV like this." His voice deepened with a sexy gruffness. His hands remained on her before he clasped them behind her back.

"I prefer this view." She leaned in to kiss him. Taste him. Devour him.

Their lips connected with quick brushes. Their grunts and moans swelled and diminished with the warm rush of their breaths. His hands pressed in on her behind, almost lifting her off his lap.

In a flurry of quick kisses and heavy sighs, they settled into a rhythm their bodies created and celebrated. She held his face, loving the feel of his skin, the stubble of his five o'clock shadow, the contours of his jaw and the strong chin.

She held on and kissed him, kissed him hard and then soft, not wanting to stop. But in slow motion he retreated until their lips no longer touched. The air cooled the heat that pulsed throughout her lips.

"Let's continue this…in my room…or yours." She lowered her hands and rested them on his chest. The hard planes of his pecs tightened and relaxed under her touch. Contact with his body fed her need for him.

"Can't." He shook his head with added emphasis.

Laxmi waited for the explanation she knew wasn't going to keep her in her happy place.

"When I invited you, I didn't want it to be a booty call. You know, jumping in and out of bed." His direct gaze didn't waver. But it added an edge of importance to his words. "I want this time to be the beginning of many. You are interesting, although more than a bit mysterious. Even secretive." He shrugged and his expression relaxed. "I'm intrigued. I want to know what you like to eat, what movie makes you cry, what invites that beautiful, megawatt grin to shine. And that's only a sample of what I hope you'd share."

Laxmi nodded. "And all those things and more will be revealed after…you know…" She wiggled her eyebrows.

Opening herself to providing answers for any and every question Dresden threw her way rattled her confidence. Habits had a way of defining behavior and her instinct to stay behind the walls she'd erected was a means of protection. To trust him was to blindly fall back and hope he'd catch her.

She wanted to trust. She wanted to give in to her heart's desire to surrender and believe in gumdrops and rainbows.

"Trust me. I want you like crazy right now," Dresden coaxed.

"Funny way of showing it." Laxmi tried not to pout. Hard not to when he seemed hell-bent on dousing her fire.

He took her hand and covered his rock-hard bulge. "Not lying, babe."

She sucked air through her teeth. "I won't be able to lead you into temptation?"

He shook his head and promptly removed her hand from the intimate spot. His eyes closed and she blew out a breath before he opened them.

"I'm not one to give up easily," she warned, despite being on the verge of a tantrum.

"That's good. I like a woman with solid determination." He lifted her off his lap to the cool empty space on the couch. "Tomorrow, you can show me what's under here." His finger slipped beneath the T-shirt's hem and brushed against her belly.

She bit her lip, flinching from the intense spark of his contact with her skin.

"Tonight, I'll send you to bed with a gentle good-night kiss." His face hovered over hers. His eyes lowered to her eager mouth, lingering with its taunt.

She closed her eyes and offered her lips.

He kissed her gently on each cheek. His hand stroked

her hair. "And I wish you sweet dreams." He scooped her up before she protested and carried her against his chest to the guest room.

"I'm not sleepy," she argued. "Far from it."

"Hot milk?"

"Only if you want it poured all over you," she warned.

"Hot cocoa?" He set her down on the bed.

"Why are you being deliberately obstinate? We're grown people. I want you. You want me. Hello." She pointed to his crotch. "Let's do this." Laxmi slid under the covers and flipped back the edge on the empty side for him. "It's an either/or situation. We do this…or… I'm leaving."

Dresden had no intention of losing control over this moment. He didn't need to have control, but he also wasn't going to let Laxmi play with his feelings. Not that he deemed his efforts a success. But he was holding his own against her sensual power.

Maybe if he hadn't felt foolish running after her at the hotel, he could trust in her 100 percent. Trust that her sudden arrival came with no plans to withdraw and run.

Although it would hurt like hell, he wouldn't stop her from not wanting to be with him.

He carefully smoothed down the cover, tucking it under the mattress. Again, his stoic expression shifted into place, not revealing what he thought of her ultimatum. "You're free to leave, but you shouldn't go." His mandate was gentle but firm. "For once, no more cut and run." He turned to leave.

The pillow hit him squarely in the back of his head.

He paused, shook his head and turned out the light. "Good night."

Laxmi fumed in the dark. Sitting cross-legged with her back against the headboard, she called him a variety of sordid names.

She remained stubbornly seated on the bed, in the dark, for several minutes. She weighed her options against her bruised ego. The petty part of her demanded she pack her bags and leave. Prove the point that she had the power to end this right here, right now.

That strategy worked if she didn't care about Dresden. And more importantly than her emotions hijacking the situation, she was determined to help Fiona get what she wanted with a conciliatory meeting between Dresden and Verona.

She owed her friend that much. Nothing left to do but stay put and imagine she was on a roller coaster. Besides, he knew and she knew that she wasn't going anywhere.

Laxmi tossed back the bedcovers and got up. She grabbed her pillow and headed down the hallway. A complete surrender wasn't in her vocabulary. A compromise to Dresden's grand plans, however, would satisfy her. For now.

Without knocking, she turned the doorknob to his room and entered. She closed the door softly and waited, listening for signs that he was asleep, and walked over to the bed. Enough light from the bedside clock allowed her to navigate her path to his bed. His sleeping form was outlined under the blanket. Lying on his side, he faced the window away from her.

Satisfied that he slept, she climbed into the bed and scooted over until her body outlined his. Carefully she placed her hand over his waist.

"This is against the rules," he said, with no signs of being roused from sleep.

"No. Not really. Along with your rule about no sex,

you said I was to go to sleep. I plan to do so…in your bed."

"Not allowed." He scooted forward.

"Wasn't in the fine print." She pressed her body closer to his, making sure to close the gap between them. "And I do plan to sleep and not molest you tonight. See, I'm not using my hands." She didn't return her arm to his waist.

His body tensed. She might not have touched him with her hands, but she willfully used her entire body to spoon against his, pressing her breasts and grinding her pelvis against him. The darkness hid her smile.

"Now, how am I supposed to sleep?"

"I don't know. You obviously didn't think any of this through. But my compromise is a win for both of us." She wiggled her hips against his behind. "Let's get some sleep, shall we?"

He muttered under his breath something that sounded like *Damn, woman*.

Dresden smiled. His worrying about Laxmi's intentions and his abilities to be the perfect partner seemed a waste of time. If he could suck the life out of his doubts, he could relax and enjoy everything that Laxmi had to offer.

Laxmi had no idea if she would sleep. Lying next to Dresden, enjoying the feel of his hard-rock frame against hers, did not induce sleep. Not even counting sheep could help this dilemma. Unless he told her to get out, she planned to dig in her heels and get some sleep.

Somewhat satisfied, she snuggled her head into his back and closed her eyes. Eventually he relaxed, maybe a hopeful sign of his surrender to her. He'd learn that any mandate he gave her would only work at her discretion.

Still, it took him a while before his deep breathing signaled that he'd fallen asleep. She, on the other hand, had to resort to exercises to calm her mind. Sleeping with Dresden shouldn't mean actually sleeping in bed, spooning him.

Laxmi awoke to the rich, delicious smell of coffee. She wiggled her nose and blinked away the sleep to find Dresden standing over her holding a fully laden breakfast tray.

"Rise and shine. Here's your yummy-for-the-tummy food." He placed the tray over her after she pulled up in a seated position.

"Thank you. I was sleeping hard." She pushed back her hair that felt like an untamed tangle around her head.

Laxmi shook her head, amazed over the complete treasure of a meal: freshly baked blueberry muffins, scrambled eggs, bacon, sliced oranges and bananas. Thanks to his offerings, she'd be set to begin a long day.

"Your little puff-puff snores let me know that you were getting the rest your body needed."

"I do not snore." She selected a warm muffin, took a healthy bite and groaned through her chewing. "And besides, if I did snore, you should be a gentleman and not mention it."

He pulled out his phone, pressed the screen and scrolled through before he started typing.

"What are you doing?"

"I'm making my list of memorable things about Laxmi Holder."

"And that made your list? What else do you have on there?"

Chuckling, he moved his phone out of her reach.

After she demolished the muffin, Laxmi moved on to the scrambled eggs and crispy bacon. She had a lot of questions for Dresden, but the food smelled good and was enjoyably hot and she didn't want to stop eating for a second.

"More coffee? Muffins? Fruit?"

He continued offering seconds, but Laxmi was getting full. However, she cleaned her plate, almost saddened that her meal would end soon.

"That was tasty. Thank you." She watched him take the tray and disappear out of the room. A happy sigh escaped. She stretched her arms and relaxed against the headboard.

"I could get used to this," she said softly to the empty room.

They stood barely a foot apart, holding eye contact, the air between them charged with high-voltage electricity. The space practically hummed and sparked. Not allowing one more second to pass, he crossed the hallway and pulled her close.

His fingers curled around the opening of her robe. "It's always my pleasure to give you what you need."

"And you know what those needs are?"

"But of course, and I darn sure know how to be your solution."

"Arrogant so early in the morning."

"Confident after a night of spooning." His eyes lit up with his teasing.

"I want you to know that you got off easy last night." She took a step back into the bathroom. Good. She still had his attention. "I'd advise that you don't use the same exit strategy." She shrugged out of the robe and let it drop to the floor to pool at her feet.

He sized her up and unrolled his sexiest smile. "Had no intention of doing so. It's a brand-new day. I'm ready to mount another campaign on your defenses." He openly admired her breasts and pert nipples that ached for him to hold, suck and stroke to her heart's content. He didn't miss the slight shiver of anticipation that shook her body.

She turned to step into the bathtub. "Care to wash my back?" She turned on the water and held her hand under the stream while adjusting the faucet until it hit perfection.

"Sure." He didn't walk toward her until she stepped into the bathtub. Then he picked up her robe and hung it on a hook on the back of the door. He took his time toying with her patience.

In response, she tilted her head, sticking out her chin in a stubborn gesture, warning him not to underestimate her.

Under the steady stream of water beating down on her head and body, she looked at him. Her nakedness didn't reduce him to shyness. He addressed her body like a man who knew that she was his. Like a man who knew how to tame her needs.

She handed him the washcloth already loaded with shower gel. "Here ya go."

He took it and added a slight bow to her. His hand guided the cloth in a series of long swipes crisscrossing her back. Her body moved to the pressure of his hand. But then he concentrated his efforts on her shoulder blades. Her back rounded, answering the attention.

The washcloth dropped to the bottom of the tub. "Oops." He reached for it.

Laxmi restrained his wrist. "Use your hands." She now faced him. "You ought to comply," she said when he didn't budge. "You started this episode. Waking me up. Exciting me. Making me wet without the use of the shower. Time to pay up."

"Tease all you want. Nothing is going to happen."

Laxmi shrugged. "Go ahead, then. Wash my body. Let's see how in control you really are."

He turned off the water, poured the shower gel into one hand and used the other to lather it into suds. Then he looked at her, as if waiting for her to change her mind.

Instead she raised her hands out on each side of her body and slightly spread her legs. No words necessary, in her opinion.

Laxmi heard his exhalation before he placed his hands on her shoulders and moved from her arms down to her hands. His nostrils flared. Lips tightened. A soft, gruff sigh hissed from between his open mouth.

Pleased to see his reaction, she didn't hide her smirk. She added a soundtrack of moans as he rubbed the gel along her breasts.

Her nipples stayed erect every time his hand made a sweep. Concentration was necessary to remain upright. He wasn't unaware of her body's response. She knew he toyed with her when he circled her breasts with the liquid soap in his hands and then quickly finished off with a soft pinch to each nipple. Her breath sucked in like a vacuum. She held it for a beat and exhaled with a loud groan.

Heat rose and blossomed in the intimate space between her legs. She no longer tried to remain cool. Excitement pulsed through every nerve, touching off a domino effect of her desire.

Now his hand splayed across her belly and finger-walked down to the landing strip to her vagina.

She looked up at the ceiling, sucking in deep breaths. Her hands pressed against the cool tiles. She closed her eyes and gritted her teeth at the sweet agony.

He didn't ease his game of sweet torture. "You sure like to play with fire." His hand closed loosely around her neck.

She gasped as his other hand slipped between her legs and his fingers slid into her. She raised on her tiptoes, her whimpers eerily echoing in the bathroom.

"I want you to come," he whispered. "Don't fight it."

She couldn't if she wanted to and—*OMG!*—she had nothing to block his way with her.

Under his power, he worked her. His fingers performed magic that drew her desire out into the open. Her breath hissed. Her willpower equally evaporated into the air.

Her tender lips were under assault by his fingers in the sweetest way. Over and over, he slid in and out of her cave, stroking her into a frenzy of erotic swirls of pleasure. Her sex vibrated from the thrill of attention. His touch pulled her deeper under his spell. She blinked rapidly to cut the effects.

He turned on the shower to a soft rain. The warm water created rivulets over and between her breasts, washing her belly. She tilted her head forward for the water to rinse her back and splash over her backside.

"Don't hold anything back." His command stayed low, a personal decree to be obeyed.

His fingers increased their play. She soared higher, faster, spinning in a state of euphoria. She gripped his shoulders to hold out. His mastery to open the gates for her release left her without words but uttering long moans of happy sighs.

"Put your hands back on the walls."

She tried, but every time he stroked and pushed higher, she couldn't think. Couldn't obey. Her nails sank into his shoulders.

"Then you'll be punished."

She dearly hoped so.

His mouth closed over hers with a brief connection as he pulled gently on her bottom lip.

Laxmi ground her hips against his hand.

His continued retreat-and-advance tactic between her legs sent her to a sphere beyond her own making.

He marked his way down her body with his mouth closing over her nipple and lapping at it with his tongue.

She looked down at him as he knelt in front of her. This time, her hands did press against the walls. The marked coolness of the tiles stemmed the fueled liftoff that was bound to happen. Otherwise, under the power of his tongue, she might as well have suffered a rocket-jet expulsion and have been brought to her knees.

The man didn't let up. He'd promised a punishment and he was dedicated to making it happen. His mouth and his fingers did equal work.

His lips suctioned onto the sensitive area and pulled her into the warmness of his tongue. He worked her into a frenzy: no pauses, no time to think, no time to breathe. Deep within her, where her desire had awakened and simmered with growing power, she recognized the brink on which she stood. Her cries echoed and blasted into the room, probably audible through the vents.

Her body shuddered a full release that rocked her all the way through her toes. Wave after wave. Tremors rolled with rippling effect, getting bigger, wider, until the release consumed her.

On the ride, she held on to Dresden, no longer caring for the cold, hard tiles. She needed his smooth skin, hard muscles, warm body. He offered up himself—his magic fingers—to pull her in and set her free.

She barely acknowledged that the water no longer poured overhead. Her senses hadn't returned to normal. She had barely touched down from the wild ride before Dresden wrapped an opulently thick towel over her shoulders and pinned it in place. Vigorously he rubbed her shoulders and arms, drying her off.

"You had what I needed," Laxmi said with a happy sigh. Her skin tingled in the afterglow.

"Always." He kissed her softly. "You can go off to work wearing your grin. Make folks wonder what's got you smiling."

"You mean who's got me smiling." She looked up into his handsome face. "And it's all your fault, Mr. Haynes."

"Guilty." He held up his hand. "And I have no remorse."

"Good." She giggled. "Neither do I. Just sexy memories to keep me blushing all day long."

Laxmi threw off the towel and exited the bathroom, comfortable in her nude state to get dressed.

"See, you still got what you wanted." Dresden leaned against the door frame, looking heated. The vein raised along the center of his forehead was the only sign of his exertion.

"Every single time," Laxmi boasted with a wink.

Chapter 9

Dresden always counted himself lucky during flu season not to be knocked flat on his back. Allergies also gave him a wide berth with no stuffy-head, runny-nose symptoms. The next morning, however, he woke consumed by a strange, unfamiliar malady—one that was less physical, but more emotional.

His central nervous system took a direct hit. A slow invasion that had Laxmi's name on it. He welcomed what she offered, despite the uneasiness of how quickly she had taken over his mind, feelings and life.

Earlier that morning he'd called in sick. It was a win-win for him and his students, who were going to have a pop quiz on the three significant periods in American history that influenced the migration of blacks to Canada. They could count themselves lucky that Laxmi had agreed to his impulsive arrangement to selfishly have her to himself.

In the crook of his arm, his woman lay curled up against his body. They'd made love until they no longer had strength beyond limply holding each other coming down from their high. He enjoyed the warmth of her body and the silky smoothness of her skin.

Having Laxmi here with him in Toronto felt good and natural. He wasn't sure what her intention was when she'd arrived in the city beyond wanting to see him, but he now wanted to open his life to her.

The Meadowses forced him to think about family, but also surprisingly about the future. His awareness of the family's news without intending to keep himself updated was the result of his unfolding relationship with Fiona and to some extent his cousins and their partners. There was a sense of community that he wanted for him and Laxmi.

Dresden slipped out of the bed for a quick shower. He emerged to see her still curled up under the covers. A gentle snore buzzed from between her parted lips. He smiled, enjoying watching her sleep. Her thick, dark hair fanned the pillow. The duvet was bunched under her arm. A bare leg poked out. He liked that she slept with carefree abandon. If he could, he'd sketch his sleeping beauty. But instead she needed a nudge to wake up.

He finished dressing and headed for the kitchen to brew a carafe of coffee. By the time he returned, he expected signs of life. Laxmi, however, still slept. This time the exposed leg was back under the cover. He set down the full coffee mug near her. As the robust scent of roasted chicory wound its way past her nose, she stirred and mumbled incoherently. Her eyelids fluttered but didn't open. Instead she rubbed her face in the pillow and burrowed deeper under the duvet.

He grinned at his beautiful sleepyhead. She obviously needed more assistance to get her out of the bed and functioning. A few kisses to rouse her would be the easy way. The fun way. The solution popped into his head. He bit down on the laugh bubbling up to betray him. This option would deliver a guaranteed curse-out by Laxmi.

With the flourish of a masterful magician, he snapped apart the drapes covering one window, then the next. The morning sun shattered the dimness in the room. He had to squint as his pupils revolted under the painful contraction. His laughter erupted at her first wail.

Laxmi's high-pitched cries attacked his eardrums before she slid completely under the covers. Her stream of words was mostly unintelligible, harsher, with a mix of guttural roars.

Oh, wait. He did recognize that physical impossibility that she wished upon him. He couldn't stop laughing.

She emerged in a disheveled fury of sexy badassness. Her hair crowned her head in a wildly off-centered style with various sections staking their own space, in their own direction. He liked it.

"I hate you. Where's my coffee?" She blinked and yawned. The scowl diminished a tad.

"Grumpy, are we? Check near your elbow." He motioned toward the side table.

"Miss Grumpy to you." She sipped the coffee and succumbed to its spell. Finally she cast a withering gaze at him. "I've nothing charitable to say to you now."

"A man's got to do what a man's got to do—getting you up and ready to go takes herculean strength." He snapped his fingers and motioned to the bathroom as if he was an airplane marshal guiding her in to the terminal gate.

"Why are you peppy? Are you always like this?" She took another sip. Her happy groan said it all. She and her coffee clearly were having several moments.

"Time's not on our side. There's a lot of Toronto to show you."

"Key question—is this tour going to get me revved up for later…in your arms…between your legs? Because that's all that matters to me."

"Yes. Yes, it will. Now move your sexy buns."

"Liar!"

"She shouts with no proof." He took her coffee mug from her hand. "Holding it hostage."

She pushed up to kneel on the bed. Her lips puckered in a sexy pout. "Mwah."

"Stop that." He had the day planned and she was already pushing it off course.

"I don't need to see Toronto. Would rather not waste a second on anything other than you."

"Duly noted. In the rules of courtship, you have to make time to learn about each other."

She frowned. "More rules? Not my thing. Besides, no need to know everything."

"Why? You've got secrets?" he teased.

"Don't we all?" She tilted her head and looked at him with a steady gaze.

"Nope. Everything is out in the open." The instant he said it, he realized he did have a secret. The depth of his feelings for Laxmi wouldn't ever pass from his lips to her ears. Still, he shook his head, maybe not as vigorously.

"Not likely. But suit yourself." She shrugged off his continued protests. "Besides, rules don't work for me. My track record kind of shows that."

"Resist all you want. I look forward to getting to know you." And he meant it.

"Okay, we can start right here." She crooked her finger, calling to him.

"I'll be in the living room." He pointed at her. "Get dressed. Please."

"Coward." She flipped off the covers, no longer shielding her nakedness.

His mind pleaded for mercy. His body reacted like a starved beast. Dresden hurried out of the bedroom. He'd no shame admitting his weakness. One more second, though, and he'd peel off his clothes and be right there hip-thrusting and grunting. The mental image of Laxmi grinning kept him from making a U-turn.

Not long after, he heard the bedroom door open. She sashayed down the hallway and past him. Naked. Her bare behind looked so damn good.

"Why do you do this?" His hand twitched with anticipation to touch her, feel her body in motion.

"Because you live by order. I live by chaos." She turned, faced him with all her naked splendor, and he just about melted.

He looked at his watch. "We'll be late for breakfast. Reservations."

"Looks like you'll have to make other plans, then. I'll be your buffet. You can eat whatever you like, and have seconds, thirds, until you're all satisfied." She smiled with cruel intent.

Dresden took a step back from her temptation and counted off on his fingers. "We have breakfast, then the anniversary of hockey at the Hockey Hall of Fame, the Winterlicious event—"

"Winterlicious? What's that?"

"It's a food festival where you can enjoy three-course meals from participating restaurants."

"Ah, like our Taste of New York City."

He nodded. "We have that for Toronto, too. But I'm not done with impressing you. Then it's poetry at Crow's

Theatre, and midnight skating." He looked up at her, sensing her body, her sensuality, which might as well be its own real-to-the-touch entity.

She lay on the couch with her leg hitched on the back of it. "I'd like the taste of Toronto right now. We can do the rest later." She rested her arm over her head and closed her eyes. The devilish smile still curved her lips.

Her evocative centerfold pose whipped his senses, sanity and emotions into a fractured mess.

Dresden would never win any arguments with this woman. If he did manage any victories, he knew it would be because she allowed him the rare treat of winning. She toyed with his willpower, bringing him to his knees.

"Come on, baby. I'm so wet for you." Her invitation curled around him like the coffee vapor he'd used to tantalize her earlier.

Dressing might have taken minutes. Undressing took seconds. Dresden's willpower snapped like a dry twig as he tossed his clothes into a heap. Seconds later, he stood over Laxmi, aroused and naked.

She beckoned to him. "Closer."

He slid into her, wet and warm. His hand grasped the sofa's arm. His fingers curled and dug in. The words he intended to say turned into a long, pleasurable groan.

Her legs wrapped and closed over his behind, tilting her hips up to him. He accepted the invite and slid deeper into her.

"You blow my mind." He hadn't let up on his rhythm.

"I hope that's not all that I'll blow." She nipped at his earlobe. Her breath tickled his ear.

Dresden gritted his teeth. He bore down and let go. His body shuddered against hers, pulsating against the tiny tremors that shook deep within her.

He lay on his side, propped on his elbow, admiring her delicate profile. He kissed her temple, nuzzling her hairline.

"I give you permission to make love to my body whenever the mood hits."

"You're beyond generous, sweet lady."

"Quite the opposite. I'm a bit selfish with whom or what I want. And that would be with you."

He kissed her just to have another taste of her mouth. His toes curled with the instant reaction of their intimate touch. He cupped her face, enjoying the softness of her skin against his hand.

"Permission to kiss me granted." Laxmi's tongue touched the tip of her upper lip. Her breath pushed out a little hard.

"As you command." Dresden laughed as she tried to kiss him but he pulled away each time.

"You're a tease."

"And you need to stop getting your way and get dressed. We have a city to explore."

"Spoilsport." She rolled out from under him and stood. "You know we don't have to go out."

Her lower half didn't need to be that close to his face. To keep his hands off her, he got up and retrieved his clothing. For the second time that morning, he got dressed to head out.

When Laxmi offered to help, he placed his hands firmly over hers. She worked visibly hard to prevent a toothy smile by biting her lip.

"Nope. You are not going to tempt me again." He stepped out of her way. "Come on. Canadian hockey awaits you."

She groaned and made a face.

* * *

Dresden loved playing tour guide. Sharing history and answering Laxmi's questions turned it into a fun event that did manage to raise her interest, too. By the end of a hockey overload, she'd suggested they attend a game to see if it was as exciting as he made it seem.

Not only did he look forward to taking her to a game, he also looked forward to planning another date weekend with her. She wasn't going to jump in her car and put distance between them. Playing the emotionally distant guy to match her philosophy took a lot out of him. He couldn't help feeling a bit giddy.

"Where to next?" Laxmi took his arm and wrapped it around her shoulders. "I'm famished."

"Next up is a late lunch." He ignored her threat. "And we can walk there. Just a few blocks down and then across."

"You are really pushing it."

"I want your appetite in full rage by the time we get there."

"It's freezing." She blew an exaggerated breath that instantly vaporized.

"Then we'd better hurry." He pinned her hand to his and set the brisk pace to University Avenue.

By the time they barreled into the hotel lobby, they welcomed the warmth with a mix of relief and exclamations of joy. Dresden took turns rubbing Laxmi's arms and blowing on her fingertips. She shivered and sniffed noisily, her teeth chattering through her smile. He kissed each fingertip, then her lips, and went back to her fingertips until her body stopped its uncontrollable shaking. And because he still wanted to touch her, he added a soft kiss on her forehead. Her whispery sigh blew against his neck. He was sinking fast.

A blast of cold, coming from patrons exiting the hotel, slammed the brakes on his desire.

"Let's go in. Once you see the beautiful setting, you won't remember that you're cold."

She rolled her eyes at him.

Dresden checked their coats and led her to the entrance.

He heard the inhalation.

"Beautiful. Calming," she whispered as she looked around the elegant surroundings.

The soft peach decor and off-white furnishings offered a soothing effect. Off to the side near the restaurant's name, shelves of ceramic vases filled the wall. Their hostess guided them to the seated waiting area where, for ambience, comfortable sofas were separated by tables with centerpieces of lit coals on low flames.

The restaurant's participation on the Winterlicious lineup had attracted many patrons. The room buzzed with conversation and social merriment. Laxmi curled into his body as they waited and he explained the Canadian and Asian influences on the menu.

Laxmi settled on the Thai Coconut Noodle soup and he chose the Bosk Burger. Between them they devoured an appetizer of crispy calamari.

"Was this one of your romantic jaunts?" she asked between spoonfuls of soup.

"Nope. I'd attended a conference on the Asian-African cultural influences in early Canadian history. We ate here for dinner."

"So you and another sexy, nutty professor never got your grooves greased after a conference."

Dresden laughed hard. "Sometimes. But it wasn't so... blunt."

"It's always that way—blunt. We just like to pretty it up with our die-hard romantic notions."

He took a minute to sip his water. "You have never fallen in love?"

"I have. That's why I know."

"But it was the wrong guy. Or you weren't the right girl."

"True. But if you don't let your heart hang out, then you don't have to worry about someone using it as a welcome mat." She finished her soup and daintily wiped the corners of her mouth.

Dresden had no idea what to ask next or what to say next without sounding as if he wanted her to admit to deeper feelings for him. To know her truth might sting a lot.

"I like you. I like being here, hanging out. But I'll be honest that I've got my heart protected. It just is what it is."

"What are you looking for in a guy? The one who will unlock that heart."

"No one is up for the job."

Dresden set aside his napkin. He looked at her, stared at her, pushing to be heard with what he had to say. "I beg to differ. Give me time and I'll chip away at that ice."

She leaned back. Her eyes lit up over the direct challenge. The corner of her mouth lifted a smidgen. "Bring it."

Dresden signaled for the check. He had accomplished many things in life. Never had he had a desire to win a woman's heart before. No one had measured up to someone he wanted for a long-term relationship with, much less as a partner for life.

Until he'd met Laxmi, he hadn't a clue who he was looking for in his life. He didn't know what he did want for himself until he couldn't stop thinking of her, craving the next minute when he could talk to her, listening to her share her dreams, or replaying moments of her smiling, walking, laughing, teasing him. Her confident sense of self and bold, fearless participation in her life more than attracted him; it communicated directly to his soul. The revelation wasn't a sudden flash. Resistance in being too invested and too desperate for a guaranteed outcome was strong and persistent. But she'd turned the key that locked away the demons which had taken up residence from the time he'd understood his adopted status, that he'd been a choice that was on the losing side, where rejection, abandonment and bitterness were roommates.

But he didn't fear failure because he didn't plan to sink in this venture. This was more than winning a bet, but merely acknowledging what he wanted out of hooking up with Laxmi.

While she might think it was his job to free her heart, he would show her that she had to do it with him supporting her. He wasn't going to wine and dine her into submission or get freaky in bed for her to say yes. The only thing he didn't know was how much time she was willing to invest in them.

"I was hoping to inhale everything on the menu." She patted her belly. "I can't eat one more thing. But it was all so good."

"We can put it on our must-do list for when you come back."

"Sounds good."

Dresden signed off on the bill and slid it to the edge of the table for the waiter.

"Let's go." He offered his hand to escort her back into the cold.

"What now?"

"Mall or movie. Then we'll eat and have a midnight skate."

"You are determined to have me work off every calorie I consume."

Dresden had planned the day with a meticulous passion. But the sudden shift of gears between him and Laxmi had him digging deep for inspiration. While she watched the movie, he racked his brain to think of ways to seduce her. Ways that would change her mind-set rather than reinforce the fear and disappointment she'd already suffered.

"Good movie." She turned down the car's radio volume to talk. "I'm impressed with your selection."

"Glad you liked it. Folks were talking it up on Twitter."

"You have an account?" She laughed. "What's your handle?"

"For that hysterical laughing, you will not get any information from me."

"So you do have secrets."

He shook his head and ignored her as he headed out of the downtown area to the suburbs.

"Where are we headed?"

"You'll see."

With Laxmi playing guessing games and getting all the suggestions wrong, Dresden didn't offer up much in clues. He pulled up into a familiar driveway and parked.

"Welcome to my home—well, my parents'."

"Oh." Her smile froze as her eyes widened. "Meeting the parents." She pulled down the visor and slid the cover over the mirror.

"You look fine. And they're not here. They're in Kazakhstan on a job." He laughed as she blew out a breath.

"A warning next time. Please." She hopped out and

looked around. "Why do I see you with your books tucked under your arm—you wearing your red sweater and Argyle socks—coming home?"

"My uniform was navy blue. Blue or black socks were the only options."

"Well, la-di-da." She mocked with her version of a snooty woman, nose in the air and hand stuck out with pinkie finger up, marching to the front door.

"Maybe this wasn't a good idea," he muttered as he followed her to unlock the door.

"Why don't you stay here? Beautiful house," she asked upon entering the foyer.

"My parents are in and out of this house. It's their base. I've moved on and like the stability of one place without the hectic motion of people coming and going."

She nodded. "I can understand that. So you have to check up on the house?"

"I come in once a week unless we have renters. Go through the mail. Water the plants. I usually have to video-chat with my mother so she can see that I have done my chores." He laughed, but loved having the zany discussions with his parents. They'd never ask him for updates about the Meadowses. At first, he didn't volunteer anything. Withholding information wasn't his intent. But he wondered if they would see any thaw in his relations with the Meadowses as a move away from them. Or, on the other hand, when he still didn't want to deal with Verona, would his mother pressure him to forgive? Deep down he knew that Charlotte expected that of him with Verona.

"Don't let me stop you from your routine. Go do your thing." She looked up the stairs. "Is your room still pristine? Like a shrine to the dutiful son?"

"Don't make fun of my mother." He pulled her hair. "And, yes, it's the third room on the right."

He'd barely finished the sentence when she took the stairs like a gym rat in the zone, pumping her arms and legs until she reached the top and disappeared down the hall.

Dresden heard the door open and close. Nothing much for her to see. His mother had kept school awards and college honors on the wall. No athletic trophies dotted his shelves, since he both couldn't play lots of team sports and disliked not getting picked to play said team sports. Instead she'd find his comic-book collection, his badges to the various conventions, and the beginnings of an obsession with history.

Dresden tried to ignore Laxmi's loud exclamations and went about his tasks. Once a month, he had a cleaning service come in to dust and vacuum. So far, he'd managed not to kill any of his mother's plants.

Why did he give Laxmi free rein in his room? He imagined her texting or posting photos of his room with snarky comments. While she probably found his teen life hilarious, he switched gears and pulled out a take-out menu.

By the time she came skipping down the stairs with souvenirs of her invasion, the Chinese food had arrived.

"Hmm. Smells yummy. And I have worked up an appetite." She helped set their places as he put the various food selections along the center of the table.

"My mother has all my stuff cataloged. She'll hunt you down in New York for any missing items."

"But you won't let her." She pouted.

"Depends if you're taking them to have something to remember me by or if you plan to have nightly laugh fests with them."

She leaned over and kissed him. "Maybe a bit of both. But I love these items. They are so you. So real."

"Here's your food."

She set the action figure to sit in front of her. "He kind of looks like you."

"Buffed and inscrutable." He did his best impression of the hard, blank face of his beloved action figure.

"You're the perfect superhero type," she mused.

"Now you're being cruel."

"Nope. It's always the quiet types that have the deepest strength. The others are brute force and brawn. Boring. The intellectuals have a delightful way of taking their time, stroking their way, biding their time to the happy ending." Laxmi had thought of Dresden in superhero terms from the first time she'd met him. And she sometimes doubted that she was the perfect fit, a support rather than a heavy weight, for him. But he'd never left her thinking that she was unworthy. Quite the opposite. He encouraged her to celebrate her own worth, regardless of what she hadn't accomplished. He was a strong ray of sunshine that warmed her.

He puffed up his chest. "Yeah. Do I need an *S* on my chest?"

"No, you need something original. Mysterious. Dark. Brooding."

"I don't brood."

"You think hard." She smiled. "Better."

"Every superhero needs a leading lady."

"Are you holding auditions?"

"Only have one person in mind."

"I wonder who that will be."

"She'll know. They always know that they are the one."

"But then they let the superhero go because he's got a destiny bigger than hers."

"Or she takes a step back out of fear."

Laxmi stopped eating and pointed her chopsticks at him. "What woman has been afraid to step up to be with her superhero?"

"Not answering." He eyed the chopsticks that snapped at him. "But you're making my point." He jumped up to dodge the fortune cookie she threw at him. "And that automatically disqualifies you, missy."

He caught the second fortune cookie, broke it, pulled out the fortune and ate the cookie.

"You are not going about wooing my heart very well," she complained.

"All in good time." He crunched on the second piece of cookie. He'd turned into a great pretender brimming with confidence and a solid sense of his life's direction. "Let's clean up and get our skating on."

The Natrel Rink at Harbourfront Centre had summoned a sizable population of the city to midnight skating. Dresden had spent many winter nights when school was out skating and hanging out with his friends. They'd talked about girls, college plans and girls again. He'd never been great with keeping in touch and neither had his friends as they scattered after graduation. Now that he was fairly settled in his teaching career, he planned to reconnect with the handful of schoolmates who'd extended friendship.

"It feels good in here." Laxmi stood close to him, recovering from the brisk, cold walk from the parking lot.

"I brought you my gloves and hat."

"I dressed for fashion, not torture." She stripped off her gloves and took his square but sturdy pair. "I'll pass on the hat."

"Now is not the time to be stubborn." He pulled off her hat before she could stop him. Then he tugged down the hat he'd brought for her, almost covering her eyes. As cheesy as it sounded, she was the perfect fit for him. She breathed a renewed freshness into his life. With her, he saw the world with a clearer perception. The sensation was a little heady, but it was refreshing to want to wake up and face the day—or, in his case, face the Meadowses.

She swore softly. "I'm already sweating under this monstrosity."

"Then it's time to get out there and skate. Shoe size?"

"TMI. I can get my own skates." She walked off in a huff.

He smiled and took off his shoes, replacing them with his personal skates. "Need help?" he asked when she returned with her pair.

She shook her head. "I've skated before. And you're hovering like a helicopter dad. I know what to do. I've got this."

Dresden didn't doubt that she had skated, but he wondered how long it had been since she'd been on a rink. Something told him to stick close to her when they stepped out onto the ice.

"Let's go." She popped up and tottered off in front of him.

At the door, he saw her visibly brace before stepping outside. Her shriek at the blast of air off Lake Ontario drew a few chuckles from nearby skaters. She looked frozen to the spot. Her eyes watered. And all he wanted to do was hold her close and kiss that pout away.

Despite the night's darkness, the rink was lit in colorful lights splashed across the ice. The constant flow of skaters, the buzz of conversation and the cool air blew away the stresses of the day. Skating was simply refreshment for the soul.

"Stop grinning and let's go. If I stand here any longer, you will have to chisel me out."

He skated toward her and slipped his arm around her waist. "Ready?"

She nodded.

He set the pace, not fast or slow. She held his hand and kept her body close to his. They moved as one, as he dearly wanted to out there in the real world. He wanted her to relax and let him lead sometimes. Then he'd share the honor with her. Like skating with a partner, trust mattered. Trust made a difference. He hoped that they would continue toward that undeclared goal. The backdrop of lit buildings against the dark sky blurred as they navigated their way around the rink.

A large crowd entered their area, slowing the momentum. Dresden looked over at Laxmi. "Need to stop?"

She shook her head. "Watch this!" With a slight push, she skated away from him toward the center of the rink. In a series of moves, she went from Laxmi the chaotic entertainment manager to a skating dynamo. She moved with the grace of a ballet dancer, but the style of a skater with mad skills. Then she spun, her body arching back, her arms gracefully arching through the spins. She took his breath away. Finally she slowed and stopped with a flourish. A small cheer went up.

"If I'd skated like that from the beginning, you wouldn't have been next to me, holding me close, getting me in a romantic mood."

Dresden bowed. "Secrets coming to light."

She laughed. "Plus, I wanted to show off to you."

"Got to admit, I was proud. Wanted to tell the crowd, 'That's my woman.'"

She laughed and he watched her breath escape into

a misty vapor. "Okay, now I'm ready to go inside and warm up."

"We can grab a hot chocolate and share a dessert."

They both sighed under the warmth of the building.

"I know you want to do midnight skating. And it's thirty minutes from midnight, but I know that after I've thawed and eaten, you'll have to lift me onto that rink. I'm done." Laxmi took the closest seat to start unlacing her skates.

"You'll get no fight from me. Haven't skated since last year. My body is cursing me out for this."

"Let's get that hot chocolate before our muscles lock up and we need a barrel of Bengay to get us moving again."

They made their way to the restaurant and got a table. After putting in their order, they sat in companionable silence. Dresden couldn't explain what he felt. Being happy sounded simple and overused. But today, he'd enjoyed every minute with Laxmi.

Their hot chocolates arrived in big mugs. He enjoyed watching Laxmi lick the whipped cream off her lips. A job he'd prefer doing under a more intimate setting.

"I've got to say that I didn't think I'd have a good time. I'm glad you brought me here. I kind of fell back in time to when I used to compete."

"You were fantastic. Why did you stop?"

She looked down at her mug, her expression partially hidden from him.

He waited to see if she would share, if she would trust him with the reason. He swirled his mug, focused on the dollop of cream.

"Couldn't get to practice. Too many hours of my life."

"But you were so good. I'm sure you have trophies."

"I won a few."

"When I visit, I want to see them."

She nodded. But there was a weak surrender that he didn't trust.

"Did you want to continue taking lessons?"

"Why should I?"

He grew impatient with her. "What part of 'good' don't you understand?"

"I'm too old. What's the point of spending all that money getting lessons for nothing?"

"Everything doesn't have to be about competition. Maybe just fun—except your skills are top-notch."

She listened to him but then shook her head. "It'll stay in the past."

"Did your parents think that you would go to the Olympics or become a professional?"

"My parents are divorced. My mother wasn't big on ice-skating." She shrugged. "Sometimes I wished that I'd never been introduced to it. Then it wouldn't have hurt so much when I couldn't go back."

"Sorry." He'd never heard her mention her parents at all. He could tell from the awkward silence that the topic wasn't a comfortable one for discussion. Like she said, he didn't have to know everything in her life. He backed away from the subject and steered the conversation onto safer land.

"No need to apologize. The important thing is that I had fun."

"Good. That makes me happy." He glanced down at her empty cup. "Need a refill?"

She shook her head.

"Then let's get out of here." He helped her with the heavy winter coat. They put on their gloves and hats, and headed back to his place.

"Got a confession," she said, her gaze averted. "You may have caused a thaw." She held her fingers up. "A smidgen."

"I've been using a blowtorch. Glad it worked." He wiped his brow as if the task had him dragging himself to the finish line.

"I'm a lot of work. May not be worth it." She shrugged. "But it'll be memorable." She offered it like a benefit for his effort.

He accepted without another thought. "Then we keep in touch. Keep this going. Upgrade a bit."

She didn't respond, didn't react. She remained neutral.

Dresden did his best not to overdo the moment. As he drove home, he chanced a few glances her way. Her head was turned toward her window. Was she thinking things over? Had he pushed a bit too hard on the last suggestion? But he wanted to know what made her so skittish.

"Upgrade?" She broke the silence with a flat, curious tone. "Like coach to business class."

"Workable analogy." He'd have jumped straight to first class. But at least she was willing to come up the aisle with him.

"We can give it a shot."

"I feel like you'll roll out terms and conditions." He was only half joking.

"I don't tend to do things with one foot in. So you might regret making me your official girlfriend."

"As unofficial girlfriend?" He never played the field. Did she?

"Nothing meant by it. It's like a green flag that you can change your relationship status for onlookers."

"My fandom will be pleased." He was again grateful that he had only read such news on Twitter and didn't contribute to it. "And yours. Anyone who may need a telegram?"

She paused a few seconds longer than he was comfortable with and then said, almost to herself, "Nah. It'd be a lost cause, anyway." She sighed and turned back toward the window.

While Dresden wanted to do spins with the car and shout out his happy news, he worried that Laxmi had retreated behind whatever history had brought on that mood tinged with sadness. He reached over and took her hand, grateful to feel her reassuring squeeze, as if in response to his concern.

"Business class," she reiterated.

He lifted her hand and kissed the back. Without a doubt, he knew he'd fallen in love with her.

Chapter 10

Laxmi was done with winter, especially since it kept her from seeing Dresden for several weeks. Enough already. After three weekends of heavy snowfall, the blue sky returned with a bright sun to help melt a few inches of the snow. As a result of the good weather, traffic picked up. Pedestrians in her hometown of Brooklyn braved the melted mess on the sidewalk to hit the supermarkets for restocking pantries.

Laxmi was ready to break free from her apartment to breathe fresh air. It was her turn to host the biweekly lunch with Fiona, a part of their concerted effort to repair and move on with their friendship. At first the fixed meetings felt hokey and awkward. But as each relaxed and rid themselves of the worry about judging of the other, the lunches had become a fun release from work.

Since the weather hadn't given her a chance to buy any substantive food for the meal, she opted for delivery from her favorite brick-oven pizzeria.

Her phone pinged with a text from Fiona that she had just pulled up and parked. Laxmi unlocked the door and returned to the kitchen to finish making chai.

The karha spice blend included the right amount of cinnamon, ginger, anise seed, among other ingredients, added to the aromatic tea. She poured the milky mixture into the cups and set them on a tray.

"Hey, I'm home." Fiona's entry was always the same followed by her bubbly laughter.

"Got the chai ready for us." Laxmi walked out to the enclosed porch that was toasty from the space heater. "Oh, hello." A man—not Leo, Fiona's man—stood next to Fiona.

"Last-minute change. Xavier is Leo's colleague, who just started at his law firm. Since I'm meeting with Grace today and he has to meet with Leo later, I'm driving him to the office." She threw up her hands and offered a sheepish grin. "Hope you don't mind." Fiona flopped onto the love seat and reached for her cup. "Mmm. This smells so good."

Laxmi mirrored Fiona's cheesy grin and shrugged. *What the heck?* She wasn't clueless not to pick up Fiona's blatant attempt to blindside her with Xavier. She guessed that, since turning down all of Fiona's attempts to hook her up after their talk about Dresden, her friend had taken bold steps to push her agenda.

Laxmi decided to go along, to avoid looking like the rude one. But when this little lunch was over, she and Fiona would have a talk.

"Xavier, good to meet you. I made chai, but if you want coffee or a soda, I can oblige."

"I'm fine. Really." He sat next to Fiona on the love seat.

Laxmi wondered how much he knew about Fiona's intentions. He looked nervous, but that could be the new job, maybe a new city. His personal details didn't matter because she wasn't interested. She'd picked whom she wanted to spend her time with and, if it was up to her, Xavier wouldn't get a second glance. Nothing wrong with him. But nothing right, either. He simply held no *umph*. And if he didn't even raise her pulse, she wasn't going to force the issue. Unlike with Dresden, when her pulse registered on the Richter scale for a magnitude-seven earthquake.

"Leo plans to introduce him to Grace today." Fiona looked smug. "Getting a foot in the door with her is always a good thing for an up-and-coming lawyer."

He looked embarrassed.

"She doesn't bite off heads anymore," Laxmi quipped for the sake of easing the guy's nervous expression.

He laughed—they all did—and some of the tension left his body.

Laxmi supposed there might be some truth in her statement, considering Grace's retirement transition and her age. She'd never had a one-on-one with Grace. After listening to Fiona's tales of the family, she was more than a little intimidated by the older lady. Even at the birthday party, she'd managed to keep to the edge of her periphery. Once or twice she'd felt Grace's gaze on her, but Laxmi had simply backtracked from her line of sight and ended up at the bar, where she'd met Dresden.

She remarked to Fiona, "You're all dressed up. Where are you heading to afterward?"

"Got to meet Dana at the office."

"All of you need a reminder about work values. It's Sunday, for goodness' sake."

"Grace is still transitioning out of the company. Officially resigned and all that, but there are a million things for her to take care of. So, she's in New York City on the weekends to avoid showing up at the office during the week. She doesn't want to take the focus away from Dana. Every time she's on deck, the veeps are running back and forth, not sure who to salute. The industry people wonder if she must give Dana hands-on knowledge. And the media begin to speculate all sorts of nonsense. So she sneaks in on the weekend."

"That's thoughtful." Laxmi had heard many stories about Grace's stern work ethic and expectations for her granddaughters. To hear this very human side to her impressed Laxmi. And she was doubly impressed by Grace's sensitivity and consideration of her grandson. She exhibited class all the way.

"Grace loves her life of her postretirement phase. Loves hanging out with Henry and lunching at the country club."

Entertaining used to be a thing Laxmi did when she'd lived in Los Angeles. Not much of that had happened after her career had tanked. Her lack of friends meant that she didn't have many visitors. Hosting Fiona and Leo lifted her spirits as her life continued its shift into a good place.

"Maybe you and Xavier could have lunch with Leo and me at the country club?" Fiona grinned. She wasn't the grinning sort. Her tough-cop demeanor tended to overshadow any sort of giddiness.

"You're dining at the country club?" Laxmi let the sarcasm drip like syrup over pancakes. She'd deal with the Xavier push in due time.

"If the reason is important enough."

"What could be so important?" Laxmi dared her to give voice to her agenda because, even though she hadn't told Fiona about her continued contact with Dresden, she was clear that she didn't need her to play matchmaker.

"Friendship. I want to make sure that my friends remain close to me and Leo."

"All two of them," Laxmi said drily.

Xavier earned a point for his snicker. But nothing more. The guy wasn't bad-looking. He could have been on the runway for New York Fashion Week. It didn't matter. Dresden scored all points for her—looks, brains and sexual satisfaction. Besides, he celebrated her as an equal, as a woman, and she didn't feel oppressed by testosterone-induced insecurities. He was the only man for her.

"Stop being difficult. Appreciate a free lunch and good company."

"What would you do for Meadows? Your legal area of interest?" Laxmi asked Xavier out of curiosity rather than a personal agenda.

"Estate administration," he responded with a prideful nudge of the chin. Clearly he expected her to be impressed.

"Leo and I fell in love under wills and trusts." Fiona looked at her with open mischief dancing in her eyes. She was enjoying this entire blind date and the blindsiding theatrics.

Lucky for her their lunch was only about an hour long, so Laxmi didn't have the urgency to shut it down.

"You know, it would be great to double-date. Leo and me. You and Xavier?" asked Fiona.

Xavier had moved beyond the stages of being nervous and awkward.

"Mmm." Laxmi didn't believe in being coy, but she wasn't in the mood to deliver a thousand cuts with an outright rejection. She wasn't in any need to window-shop for a man. Her life was pretty full with the perfect one.

"I think you'd make a fun couple. You're zany. He's nerdy."

Laxmi almost choked on her tea. *Wrong couple. Wrong nerd.* Although she did wish for a time when she and Dresden could double-date with Fiona and Leo.

The idea popped into her head and made itself comfortable. From everything she'd learned from Dresden, about Leo's role in finding him and how Leo had reached out to him afterward, Dresden would have no problem with growing a friendship with the lawyer. But the "happy couple" scenario of her and Dresden felt solid and good. She couldn't disregard the feelings. Sooner or later, the right opportunity would come to tell Fiona.

"Can't stay much longer. Gotta meet with my little cousin, who's trying to keep that crown on her head straight."

"Must be quite a burden. I hope she finds it worthwhile." Laxmi didn't want to think about Dana's stress level. It was one thing to start your own company and grow along with it. But to be handed over a massive business and have everyone's expectation set at the highest bar would have her eating antacids all day long.

"For her it is. She was the only one who wanted and was qualified to step into that job. But she normally doesn't work on Sunday. Thanks to Kent, who makes sure that she keeps some perspective," Fiona said.

"That's what a good man is supposed to do," Laxmi agreed, and she could now say that she had a bit of experience with a good man. His thoughtful approach to his own life guided her on how to approach her life, with its potholes and speed bumps. The way he showed his respect for her dreams and vision strengthened her resolve to do her best. More than that, his kindness to her, to his students, to Tonea, touched her, inspiring her to be of the same mind-set. She credited his parents for raising such a strong man. One day, she hoped to meet them.

"Before I go, may I use your bathroom?" Xavier raised his hand.

"Sure. Down the hall, on your right." Laxmi mirrored the directions with hand signals.

"We'll try not to talk about you while you're gone." Fiona finished with a laugh.

He suddenly looked as if he wanted to return to his seat.

Laxmi waved him on. Poor guy. "Stop teasing him," she scolded Fiona.

Of course, the minute he disappeared Fiona leaned over and whispered, "He's adorable."

"Not really. And since when did you become the romantic? Trying to fix me up, for heaven's sake, with this kid who needs to get his sea legs under him just with working in the city. Where did he come from?"

"What's got you so cranky?" Fiona hadn't stopped scowling since Laxmi spoke. "He's a good guy. Yes, he's a babe in the woods, but you are just returning yourself. You could be nice—hard for you, it seems—and show him around. Nothing major. Was only looking out for you. Don't want you walking away from a good thing like I almost did with Leo."

Laxmi struggled with how to make her point without blurting her strong feelings about Dresden.

"It was an on-the-job romance." Fiona scrunched her nose. "Messy. So I pulled the plug. Figured I was giving him space. But I couldn't forget that man. Caving in to fear was the biggest mistake I made. Had to work to get him back."

"Really?" Laxmi hadn't known the fine details of the

breakup. By that point, she'd stopped communicating with most of her friends.

"Trust was broken." Fiona sighed. "And I didn't know he was trying to find my brother. That put a twist on the relationship when I realized the real reason that Grace had him at the Hamptons during our family vacation. Trust and secrets are death notes between a couple." Fiona covered her mouth, but couldn't stop the laughter from bursting out. "I don't mean to sound like a philosopher."

"I agree with everything you said, though. When you know he's the right one, you do what you have to do."

Fiona nodded. She pointed at Laxmi and leaned in for a conspiratorial whisper. "Don't wait too long for the right one while you're setting your life on track." She looked around. "This condo is a good investment. You've got your business. You're like an eligible bachelorette. Just need to get a few more plants in here." Fiona pointed to corners of the room for the proposed greenery.

"I'm not home long enough to have plants." She took a breath and rushed on. "Especially now that I'm going to Toronto more often."

"For Tonea? Sounds like she really hit the right note upstate. And why not? It's not far from home. Yay for her." Fiona drained her cup and smacked her lips, making a thumbs-up gesture in exaggerated gratitude.

"We're considering more shows in Canada." Laxmi took another sip of her chai. As they talked about good men and love, this renewed friendship encouraged her to share the secret that lay quiet and protected from the unknown. She looked over at her friend, who happily sipped and sighed over her tea. Xavier was still in the bathroom. And she didn't want to hold on to her secret any longer. "But that's not why I'll be going there more often. I-it's…because of…Dresden."

"What?" No sign of Fiona's bubbly laughter.

"Remember when I went to Toronto for Tonea's gigs?"

"Yeah."

"I ran into Dresden."

"Really? You tripped over him on the street." Still no sign of a smile from Fiona, although her voice ticked up a notch.

"I went to his classroom. He'd left messages for me to contact him. I didn't plan on it after what we'd talked about what you wanted. But then…"

"Then…what? You figured, 'To heck with Fiona's feelings. I'm not done playing around.' And you went to him for a booty call."

Laxmi's face flushed with embarrassment. What had started as such was no longer the case. It wasn't the case by the end of the first night that she was with Dresden and it wasn't when she went to Toronto. Yes, she still sported a guilty conscience because her feelings were not yet out in the open for dissection. But Fiona had no idea how far from the truth she happened to be.

"That's it? I'm right? Oh, my gosh, you have no—"

"It wasn't like that. And I don't know what prompted me to go see him. Yes, I like being with him in that sense of the word, but I also like being with him as in talking and enjoying his company. I didn't take advantage of him, if that's what you're thinking. And he didn't of me."

"But I called you when you were in Toronto. You were with him then?"

Laxmi nodded.

Fiona's silence came hand in hand with her anger. A wall between them swiftly built up, like jigsaw pieces fitting together, and it was more formidable than the situation called for. Her friend looked at her and then away, her mouth in a tight dash of displeasure.

Laxmi tried for the calm approach. "Why is this so bad? I understand you don't want anything to go wrong with Dresden. But one of the reasons I did go to him was to help you."

"Help me? Oh, this is rich. Let's hear this crazy tie-in."

"Excuse me? Is everything okay?" Xavier hovered in the doorway.

"Thanks for coming, Xavier. Not quite the right time, though."

"It's the perfect time," Fiona snapped. "He's real. Right here. Interested." She showed off the young lawyer like a prize at a TV game show.

"Since you are determined to make your point, then so am I. Dresden and I get along. We are learning about each other and that makes it all exciting. And I know that he very much is all about family, even the Meadowses. He's coming to terms with a lot of his feelings that he didn't think he had, but he knows that they are there in him. And I think I can reach him to work through it so that he would want to meet with Verona one day." With all her heart, she would try to heal the emptiness that had burrowed deeply into Dresden's heart.

"All of this you have figured out and signed up to do without my permission."

The blistering accusation stung Laxmi's pride. "This was a favor for a friend."

"Um… I'm going to leave." Xavier pointed toward the door but looked over at Fiona.

"Stay." Fiona turned her anger back to Laxmi. "Um… since when would I ask you to get into bed with someone to encourage them to do something for me?" Fiona sucked her teeth. "Listening to you, I am more amazed that you actually believe you have those kinds of powers. I guess since you'll be so good at manipulating his feelings, then you'll be able to make him love you."

Her friend's targeted insults shot and landed deep under Laxmi's skin. The pain spread and blanketed her body, but she wasn't going to play the victim. In a weird, mixed-up way, facing Fiona's wrath helped her work out the strong emotions that consumed her.

"I do hope he loves me, and not because he feels manipulated."

"Oh, my goodness, you've fallen in love with your fantasy. Now, I'm out of here." Fiona picked up her pocketbook.

Xavier had edged toward the door. "I'll be in the car. Nice meeting you." He was gone before either one calmed down to talk.

"I'd rather you didn't leave until we clear this up." Laxmi refused to believe that she'd done something wrong. If she had been able to convince Dresden to call Verona, Fiona would be hugging her with appreciation. Instead her friend accused her of terrible things.

"Why should I stay? You kept this from me for…what? How long? A month?"

"Because I wanted to share the good news."

"No! You knew that you were in this for you—" Fiona pointed at her "—and you didn't have the guts to say so."

Laxmi bristled under the accusation. Yet there was that uncomfortable truth that she hadn't shared her romantic liaison because of fear. And she certainly hadn't shared with Dresden Fiona's strong objection to her getting romantically involved with him, just in case, under the stark analytical light, he agreed with his sister.

"What's your deal?" Fiona stood with her purse firmly over her shoulder. She stared down at Laxmi. "Are we all puppets on your stage? Is that how you think you're going to get your life back together? Manipulating them? Is Tonea's dream hers…or yours?" Fiona stepped out of the way of the love seat. "Stop meddling in my family's business."

The front door slammed.

Minutes passed before the anger in the room dissipated, before Laxmi could stop replaying Fiona's words, before her doubts reminded her that she'd set her dreams too high—first with Tonea and then with Dresden.

She'd taken it all in. She could have railed about what she'd done for the cause. She could have defended her honor. She could have written a dissertation on her love for Dresden.

The one friend who had faith in her had just pulled up the stakes and ripped apart the tent that covered them in sisterly bond. Now she sat with the cup of cold chai between her hands, fighting back tears.

Laxmi avoided Dresden's calls all day. She knew the longer she waited to take them, the more she would have to explain why she wasn't talking to him.

But this was a problem she had to solve on her own. Besides, she couldn't tell him that Fiona didn't want them to see each other. Because she would have to explain about her working to get him to meet with Verona.

Already these secrets invaded her world. And now, once they were in, they threatened to multiply faster than she could control the situation. But she wasn't ready to let go of Dresden, wasn't ready to let go of their bond.

She opted for a long walk around the neighborhood. The fresh air would do her some good. She needed time to clear her thoughts.

Laxmi grabbed her coat and set off for a brisk walk.

She headed toward a major avenue, strolling past the brownstones, crossing the street where a plethora of small cafés and boutiques lined the way. Delicious, savory smells of food and baked goods tantalized her. Restaurants were always doing good business with local residents and those wanting a quick getaway from Manhattan. Her stomach grumbled, calling out for the various foods, but she had no appetite for small crowds and officious waitstaff.

Her phone rang. It was Dresden. This time she answered. "Sorry, I've been missing your calls."

"I was getting worried. Couldn't remember if you had gone on a trip or if you were still in Brooklyn. My imagination got away with me." He laughed. "Are you okay? You sounded a little off."

"A long day, nothing more."

"No. I can hear something in your voice. You know I'm a good listener."

"I'm outside. Taking a walk."

"It was that bad? Well, you walk and I'll listen."

No matter how bad Laxmi felt, she wasn't going to tell Dresden everything. Instead she stuck to the subject of Tonea.

"What about Tonea? Do you think that I am projecting my dreams on her? Do you think that I am trying to relive my career through her? I know it sounds odd that I'm thinking of these things, but a part of me believes this."

"Whoa! Where is this coming from?"

Laxmi paused for an ambulance and its wailing sirens to pass. Maybe having this conversation outdoors wasn't the best plan, but she didn't want to be within the solid walls of her apartment, feeling like her world was closing in. She kept walking away from her condo.

"Talk to me, babe. What has you so upset?"

She blew out a shaky breath, blinked back the tears and the nerves. "It's the beginning of a new week. I was going over my schedule and my last conversation with Tonea. And it all felt like a farce. Like, who am I to do any of the things that I said I'd do? If I don't believe in it, why should she? What if she does walk?"

"Look. I'm going to be brutal. Is your business Tonea or is your business managing singers' careers? Small picture versus big picture."

Laxmi had formed her business around Tonea. She hadn't thought about managing before she'd met the young woman. Everything musical, labor and love, had been poured into Tonea.

"You can spread yourself thin managing a lot of people. But you won't have a business, either, with one client."

"You're right. I've got a lot to think about."

"And stop beating yourself up. You've got this."

"Whatever this is." Laxmi wished she could hug him for his kindness. "I miss you."

"Miss you, too, babe." He groaned. "I've got to run. Will call you later."

She hung up and held her phone to her heart. Now if he could solve her blowup with Fiona, she'd be thrilled. But any mention of Verona would guarantee a when-hell-freezes-over response from him.

With one problem given another perspective, she was ready to return home. The fine drops of snow currently falling were predicted to become a whopper in a few days. Time to stock up on savory soups, bread and hot chocolate. Laxmi retraced her steps home, adding a few stops for gathering supplies for the pantry.

All she wanted to make her first snowstorm of the year a nice one was Dresden. She tried not to let it get her down. They had managed their long-distance relationship without drama. She'd try not to whine as she was snowbound in her condo.

Chapter 11

Dresden might as well have been summoned to the principal's office instead of Grace's home, despite the backdrop of a beautifully landscaped garden. The heated solarium provided a wonderful view without the nasty bite of frigid temperatures. On this visit, there wouldn't be time to appreciate the interweaving cobbled paths and tiered arrangements for the flower beds. Or so he thought, considering he didn't know why she'd called with a Saturday-morning invitation to come to breakfast.

But like all the Meadowses before him, he suspected, he'd said, "Yes, ma'am," and arrived punctually for his appointment. Now that he was here, he wished he'd ignored Grace's request to keep the meeting private and had brought Laxmi with him. What would Grace have done? Turned her away at the door? A tiny voice in his head chirped, *Yes*.

"Thank you for coming." Grace entered the room with a style matching her name.

Dresden stood until she took her place at the small table and then took his seat. All his parents' lessons on etiquette felt like they were emerging from a dusty cupboard for his use today.

Grace always looked neat. Her clothes reflected sophistication and high fashion. Her demeanor and style were on point. But what struck him about her was that from head to toe, nothing was ever out of place. Today her hair was swept back into a simple ponytail. Every strand was accounted for and combed with military precision into place. The glasses she wore had no frames around the lenses that might detract from her general attractiveness as an elder with class. While he opted for T-shirts and slacks or sweatpants in the comfort of his home, Grace looked ready for an interview alongside Martha Stewart.

They exchanged pleasantries and he updated her on his parents' latest foray in Kazakhstan. Talking about them and the status of their project made him realize that he missed them and missed being part of the adventures around the world. Mostly he missed not sharing his fall into the well of love for Laxmi. They would have loved hearing about his roller coaster of emotions.

"You've had a wonderful education beyond books and classrooms." Grace set her teacup primly back onto the saucer. "I think it's very important for children to learn in a variety of ways. If they can't travel, then the library should be stocked with the best that the world can offer for those curious, young minds."

Talk about family and togetherness made him uncomfortable. His thoughts meandered with possibilities behind the invitation. Maybe she had finally reached the point that she was ready to talk honestly to him.

"What do you want from life?" she asked.

"That's a big question." And an answer Dresden wasn't sure he was willing to share, if he knew.

"At your age, I knew what I wanted. World domination." She laughed and he saw the gutsy, brash woman who defied the odds with her young age, race and business acumen to shatter ceilings among the corporate elite. "And I did everything to get there. Sometimes too much." Her eyebrow quirked, but her features revealed nothing further to the statement. She continued. "Mind you, I did all this with Henry probably wishing he hadn't married me. I was barely a wife. Too busy transforming into a head of my company."

"A harsh assessment," Dresden interjected then added for clarification, "Men have handled being husbands, fathers, businessmen with society's help. No one pays much attention to a man's success beyond milestones in the corporate world. He's not weighed down with the expectation to be a nurturer. Women tend to be faced with that dilemma or answer about why they selected one over the other."

"Oh."

Grace's surprise struck a funny note for Dresden. He coughed away his laugh. "My apologies. I've heard that issue tossed to my mother more than my father too many times during their careers. Some thought I was missing out on a normal life of the average kid. This woman who was overeducated, in their estimation, had her child bouncing around on camels in the desert or digging ice holes with Inuits or mountain hiking in Mongolia. I was a wild child who needed to be in the Western world to learn my proper identity."

"Normal life. Average child." Grace waved her hand. "Vague words that mean nothing. Were you loved? Were you taken care of? Were there good memories? Life isn't supposed to be all roses and gumdrops. Otherwise you wouldn't know how to handle disappointments and rejection. Life is there to teach you how to appreciate when good stuff does happen and learn the lessons necessary to keep your back straight and your chin high."

She leaned forward and her eyes squinted as she locked gazes with him. "The truth is that the labels of mother, wife and CEO aren't all that different from one another. That's why some darn good women would make ideal heads of companies."

"I agree."

"I made a darn good CEO."

"Here's to you." He raised his teacup, ready to acknowledge Grace's remarkable fortitude. Frankly, he found her self-assessment refreshing. He wondered how much he was like Grace or Fiona. Or even Verona. Maybe, over time, he could separate how he was raised from the natural traits and tendencies from his biological family.

"To mothers," she said and raised her teacup in the toast.

Dresden sipped his tea. There were mothers, and then there were good mothers. Of course, he'd expect Grace to have included all her daughters. He, however, had a mental notation to put an asterisk next to a list of good mothers. He wanted to specify Charlotte. And Grace. And even Laxmi's mother, whom he didn't know and had never met. But to include Verona in the toast was a stretch. Maybe under some other category for which that wasn't the criterion, as her son, he could give her the blue ribbon.

"Well, all the celebratory toasts must include Henry for his support and love. Henry hung in there when I went off, excited and hungry to prove my worth to the industry then to the world. I treated him as if he had no option."

"Not true." Henry interrupted as he slowly approached

the table, aided by his cane. He waved off Dresden's assistance. Without the labored walking, Henry would have defied age. His hair, cut low, was peppered with gray. Barely a wrinkle indented his skin. But it was his attitude that pushed aside any stereotypical leanings toward old age.

"Really? Do tell." Dresden knowingly took the bait with Henry's sense of humor. Besides, he appreciated how the older man's presence diluted the increasingly personal tone that had taken over the meeting. Unexpected, but equally disorienting, since he didn't know if this was Grace's style or if his visit had caused the reaction.

"Yes, Henry. What are you saying?" Grace took another sip of tea.

"Simply complimenting you." Henry opted for coffee and heavily doctored it with cream. "I wanted your success as much as you did." He looked over his glasses at Dresden and shook his head. "It was never a burden."

"See, that's why I married that wonderful man. He will defend my honor to the end. Some call it a burden, others a labor of love. But it was life. And it's why I asked you at the beginning of your visit, what do you want from life?"

"I like being a research professor. I've long settled in Canada, but I know that my job may take me elsewhere. I like being a lecturer on history and I plan to continue writing for trade journals and will eventually work on a book. But that's my life now and the foreseeable future. Not much more." His life compared to hers and what they'd accomplished in the same breath of years were at stark opposites of the spectrum.

"I'm impressed." Grace looked over at Henry, who also nodded. "'Not much more,' he says. You're doing what you love. Heck, that's half the battle."

"Don't set love aside for the ideal time, though," Henry admonished. "Don't try to compartmentalize every part of your life. It's supposed to be messy and jumbled."

"Henry. What kind of advice is that?"

"The truth. You know our lives were messy."

"Complicated," Grace corrected with a disdainful sniff. "But Henry's right—if you have someone, don't hold back."

"Do you have a special someone?" Henry asked.

Dresden nodded. He had muddled through the personal aspects of Grace's life. Foraging into unknown territory about relationships had him wishing for something stronger than tea. His mother couldn't nail him down to talk about his personal life, much less Grace, who didn't seem to talk about things without an intention.

"Don't put off the important things in life." Henry pointed to Grace as if she epitomized his argument.

Dresden couldn't deny the love that flowed between the two. To witness the deep respect and admiration was moving. He'd seen it with his parents. A special space that was beyond his inclusion, although he didn't doubt their love and acceptance of him. This unique thing— true love—seemed to hit rarely.

"I would love to meet your girlfriend."

"Grace!"

"What? Why do I need to be reprimanded? Okay, your boyfriend?"

"Grace!"

"I'll extend your invitation to her," Dresden interjected before she continued with more options.

"Wonderful. I look forward to getting to know you… everything…well, whatever you'd like to share." Grace laughed.

For the first time she sounded nervous and unsure.

The imposing figure disappeared. And a gentle, older woman with so many of life's lessons stepped into place to have tea with him.

She clasped her hands together, leaned forward and said, "With my leaving the business behind, I'm a woman focusing all my energies on the family. Better late than never."

Dresden tried to sift through every statement for clues.

"Part of my focus has been in tightening the bonds of the family. Not only by getting the younger generation interested in Meadows Media, but also supporting each other. We are one family under the name and I don't tolerate any sibling skirmishes or cousins' petty dramas."

"Not that there is any such drama," Henry clarified. "I'm proud of what my daughters and granddaughters have accomplished. They make me want to shout to the world how wonderful they all are."

Dresden nodded. He wasn't so overcome with adulation for one particular Meadows, but he wasn't going to have that conversation with the two biggest cheerleaders of the family.

"I have decided, but waited to share with you, some important news." Grace's smile dazzled him.

"This is not about bribing you—" Henry started.

Alarms rattled Dresden's nerves. Uneasiness crept in, masking the happiness he'd just felt. He'd let down his guard.

"Now, dear, you're jumping ahead of the discussion," Grace scolded her husband. "Don't mind him," she said to Dresden before she cleared her throat and tried to set her expression into a casual, friendly mask. It didn't work. "Once I knew that you were…existed, I included you in my will. You're my grandson. And no matter what, I had to do this for me. You'll be given equal shares to match all of the other grandchildren, along with a set amount of funds going into an account every quarter." She slid him a paper with a breakdown and a grand total that made him hold his breath from the shock.

No. This was much too fast. Too sudden. It was like the viral videos of a person who was knocked over by a wind gust and couldn't quite get their feet planted to remain upright.

"Wow. I don't know what to say." Dresden tried to say more but he couldn't get out why he was reluctant or, more like, horrified. The shock continued to register throughout his body. Grace had done her part to welcome him into the fold. And he tried to accept her invitations, but couldn't quite be as generous of spirit as she had. Now she'd taken her generosity to tangible levels without demanding anything from him, leaving Dresden to feel a bit ashamed, but also pressured to act nobly.

"I know this is a shock. But I chose today to tell you because I didn't see the need to wait any longer. The others wanted me to wait. Afraid that you wouldn't see this for what it was—including you in the family. And it won't be a public thing. Fiona wasn't happy with the birthday speech. But I was too proud to hold my tongue. My sincere apologies for my rambling tribute to you." She finally stopped talking, as if realizing he hadn't said much.

"I can't accept your gift." He looked down into the half-drunk, now cold tea. "Thank you for thinking about me. I just can't do it. Take your money."

"Oh, no. Henry?" Grace's voice rose.

Dresden suspected that she wasn't used to someone pushing back her forward march. And he also suspected that the ease of money flow made Grace confident that she'd get what she wanted. He'd never lived in such a world. And being given that type of access to their world didn't sit well with him.

"Son, it's not meant to be a way to bring you closer to the family. Even if you refused it, the gift is still yours." Henry did his best to add his softer touch. "And it's not about supplementing what you do in your career. This money we earned is a legacy for our family and you are part of us. It's not meant for us. We have what we need."

"Exactly. I'm not setting conditions. I want to do this. Please say that you'll accept," said Grace.

"You really don't need my yes." Dresden resisted giving his vocal support. Maybe guilt stopped him. Here he was trying to be distant and unemotional about his inclusion. It worked because they had left him alone. Now Grace pulled away the boundary he'd erected with this massive gift. He didn't know her net worth, but he knew it had more zeros and commas than he'd ever seen in his bank account.

The Meadowses' wealth drew no resentment from him. His parents' lifestyle and rich, diverse global experiences had offered a loving childhood that left him wanting for nothing. The side-by-side comparisons of the two families couldn't change his mind that he'd gotten the better deal. He'd much rather a mother who didn't regard him as inconvenient.

"I know I don't need your assent. But that's not how I do things with the family. No secrets," said Grace.

"Except for me." That shot out in a bitter tone Dresden instantly regretted.

"Yes. You were the big secret. And once I knew, I made sure to find you. No matter the outcome, I had to let you know that you do have additional people who care about you."

"I had no idea what to expect when I came here today. For days, I wondered why you wanted to see me."

"You are my grandson."

"Still, I'm not used to receiving calls from you. I worried about what we would talk about, if you would judge my answers, judge me."

"You worried unnecessarily. I only judge people after the third visit," Grace said with dry humor that left her audience wondering if she was serious or not. Her slight smile was his clue.

"I'd advise spacing out the next two visits," Henry quipped, mixing that with a throaty laugh.

"Look, I'll have to think about it. This is blindsiding—good or bad, it's a lot to digest."

"No problem. The paperwork is finalized and with the lawyers." She shrugged. "I'm not going to live forever. I don't want this to have been a wish that must be dealt with after I'm gone. Henry might take your stash and head for Vegas."

They laughed, dishing out details of what his wild nights at Vegas would entail. Before they got too outrageous and made him blush, Dresden raised his hand.

"Well, I hate to dash off. Have to meet with friends in an hour." Dresden had arranged a beer night with colleagues he knew in the city just in case he needed to pull the plug on the evening. It looked like he didn't have to commit to another event, but at least he had come prepared.

"I'm glad you didn't cancel." Grace's smile softened any hint of a criticism.

Dresden said his goodbyes and left the Meadowses' residence. He hadn't been lying when he'd admitted not knowing what to expect. If he'd had any inkling that this had been connected to the will, he wouldn't have come.

Since he hadn't known anything about Grace's methods, he couldn't help wondering if this was how she played to win.

But win what? He had already been privately and publicly introduced as the missing grandchild. Through Fiona's insistence, he'd participated in key family gatherings. There was nothing else that Grace needed from him.

Verona.

Dresden clenched his jaw. This maneuver had better not be Grace's mama-bear approach to helping her daughter. Like Charlotte, Dresden suspected that Grace had deep hopes for him to reconcile with Verona. She'd been the bad guy in his head and heart for so long that he couldn't see her in any other light. He wanted to know that the decision ate her conscience. Because if she could go on with her marriage and raising a second child without ever thinking of him, he'd suffer another letdown. Maybe he was over-thinking Grace's gesture and what she ultimately wanted. Nevertheless, he'd proceed with an abundance of caution, even if he was an instant millionaire.

Chapter 12

Laxmi breathed a sigh of relief. She and Tonea had made it. The train pulled out of Grand Central on time and headed for Boston. The car was filled on the Wednesday afternoon with every seat taken. Still, it was the better option than driving for this necessary business trip.

Since Laxmi would need to talk to Tonea, she didn't opt for the Quiet Car. The downside for where they sat was that a noisy din hung like a low cloud over the passengers with nowhere to escape and think.

"I can't wait for the time when I'm driven to my next gig. And I don't mean by you," Tonea grumbled. "This is getting old." She pouted as she looked out the window.

Laxmi knew the rant was only beginning. Her client had been particularly crabby lately. Her excitement seemed to take another dive after each scheduled activity. Just about everything drew her criticism. But when Laxmi pushed for a reason for her dissatisfaction, or any suggestions she'd like to offer to better her circumstances, Tonea stayed quiet.

"Why aren't we going to stay overnight?" Tonea pulled out her earphones from her pocketbook. Her signal that soon she'd shut Laxmi, along with the rest of the train car, out of her life.

"No need to add to the expenses." Laxmi made sure to include Tonea on the accounting side of the business. Not only should she understand what it financially took to get her career going and stay relevant, but she should also develop some sense of fiscal responsibility. When she had pulled in a few dollars in the beginning, she'd blown it on clothes or jewelry. Loaning her money wasn't going to help her learn how to be accountable to her own goals.

"I might stay overnight." Tonea dangled her earphones on one hand and scrolled through her iTunes list with the other.

"Your choice. But that means we'll have to buy new return tickets."

"Oh, you don't have to stay." Tonea continued scrolling.

"We can't use these." Laxmi pulled out the tickets. "See. Reserved. They are only good for this day."

"I know they are reserved." Tonea rolled her eyes. "I'm saying that you don't have to buy a new ticket. I'll stay in Boston. You can go back." She flicked her hand like a queen to her subject.

"By yourself?" Laxmi turned in the seat to face her. *Has this girl lost her mind?*

"Hello… I'm an adult."

"I know." But sometimes Laxmi admittedly did forget that fact.

"Besides, I'll be here with Phil."

"You do not have time to deal with a guy who is hanging on like a groupie from gig to gig. Doesn't he have a job?"

"He works. But he wants to be supportive of me. And I like having him around. Gets lonely out here." She turned away and again looked out the window, although there was no scenic view to admire.

Laxmi wouldn't pretend she didn't know what Tonea felt. A career based on hitting one venue, then another and another, from city to city, state to state, was nomadic. A suitcase or two was always packed, ready for the next gig. Saying goodbye to loved ones was never easy, but it became part of the lifestyle.

She knew that her client struggled with the loneliness. Sometimes she managed to defuse the doldrums by hanging out, chatting or going to movies after the show. But that postconcert routine realistically couldn't be for every event.

Maybe that vulnerability left Tonea wide-open for someone like Phil to pop in and take over. Ever since he'd shown up in Toronto, a change had come over Tonea. Not only was she restless, but she wasn't focused on the goals they'd set.

Discipline was always the element that was a work in progress with Tonea. There was a fine balance between motivating but not coddling her and giving in to her excuses.

Having to deal with her change of attitude and petulance had them sniping at each other, more than usual. Laxmi had expected the norming of relations after the honeymoon period. However, Tonea's attitude about the business and her career shifted into a dangerous state of casualness. Laxmi found the current status worrisome.

"Does Phil want to be a singer?" Laxmi asked. She

was always seeking what angle Phil was going after with Tonea.

Tonea laughed. "Nah. He just likes to hang around the scene. He's like one of those guys who looks at a computer and wants to dig inside to see how it works. See if he can make it better."

"Oh." *What the heck does that mean? What grown person just hangs around but is not interested in pursuing the art? And make what better?*

"He's like a world scientist." Tonea's pride oozed all over Laxmi's irritated nerves.

Laxmi blinked. *More nonsense.*

"He has a special way of looking at the world. At people. Even you."

"Me?"

"He wants to know what makes you tick. What makes me tick. What makes me want to wake up every morning and do the same thing?"

"Ah…okay." What else could she say?

"He's got me thinking about stuff lately." Tonea shrugged and turned her attention back out the window.

"Your career is like an A and B conversation—you and me. I need to know how far Mr. Phil has made it into our conversation."

"I can tell you have a boatload to say about him. But he's really cool. And, right now, he's making me happy. So we're gonna hang together after the show and then hop the train back in the morning." Tonea folded her arms across her chest and looked straight ahead. Her jaw set, as if she was waiting for Laxmi's resistance.

But Laxmi said nothing for now and let it go.

Once a week she had an official meeting with Tonea. They talked over her schedule, but also any issues that needed resolving before it got out of hand. Added to the next agenda would be Tonea's commitment to their game plan.

Laxmi wasn't of the mind-set to create a plan and be dictatorial about keeping it. However, she also didn't want to waste time pursuing a goal with no player in the game.

"You could have told me your plans earlier," Laxmi said.

"My bad. You're right. Sorry, I wasn't anticipating you being all crazy over it."

"I'll do my best not to sound unstable," Laxmi joked. But she wondered if she was the one changing. She'd never had a tiff with Tonea beyond whether she should wear a pantsuit or a dress. And she never got on her case if she missed rehearsals or gave in to feeling lazy. Frankly, with how nervous she was with her shows, Laxmi treated her with more care than she probably should have.

"Just don't want to disappoint you," Tonea remarked.

"You're doing this for you." Laxmi patted her hand. "Remember that. It's what you want that is important. And that's not the first time you've heard me say it." And Laxmi sensed that it wouldn't be the last time she would have to say it, either.

"Yeah, I know." Tonea fiddled with her iTunes and pushed the button. Conversation over.

Laxmi turned her attention to her phone as she answered emails, laying down more groundwork as planned. Now she worried about her efforts. Maybe it wasn't good enough. Maybe she had to push harder or make something big happen, sooner than later. Maybe time was running out for her to impress Tonea that she could launch her career.

Dresden thought he could escape the snowy weather in Canada. January ushered in snowstorm after snowstorm with a vengeance. He was tired of the white stuff.

Just his luck that the day he'd decided to head to New York City, the region got hit that evening with several feet of snow.

The good thing out of the snowed-in lifestyle: he'd be stuck with Laxmi in her condo. After hearing the sadness in her voice when they'd spoken on the phone about Tonea's situation, he'd booked a flight to surprise her with a visit.

Of course, he hadn't bothered to look at the weather forecast. And now he'd be in New York for the next two days. Not a bad way to enjoy alone time with his woman.

"I still can't believe you're here," Laxmi said from the bedroom doorway before going airborne to jump next to him on the bed.

"I only did it to add to my frequent-flier miles. This isn't about you." He wrapped his arm around her as she slid closer to him and snuggled against his body.

"I don't care. I'm still glad that I have you all to myself." She rested her head against his chest.

Just being close to her sent his body into hyperdrive. Their days apart made the times they were together that much sweeter. But he hated saying goodbye. Hated to sound whiny about when he would see her again.

One of his internal rules was never to pressure her. They weren't the only couple in the US and Canada with a long-distance relationship. People survived the miles and often lived and loved better than couples in close proximity. Or so he kept telling himself.

These precious shared moments were what mattered, here and now. He pulled her close until her heartbeat could be felt against his body. Her leg lay across his. He enjoyed her warmth.

"I loved waking up to you making love to me this morning," she said.

"Can't get enough of you." He meant that to his very soul.

"When I'm with you, nothing out there exists. Feels unimportant."

"Too bad we need money, food and comforts, or we could be like cave dwellers and live on the land." Dresden wished he could be cavalier and impulsive, unlike the reality of his micromanaging of his own life.

"I like the scene. Skinny-dipping in the nearby lake and putting on our leaves for when we have company."

Dresden chuckled, along with Laxmi. Instead of their fantasyland, they would be right here in Brooklyn waiting out the storm in each other's arms. Not a bad way to spend a few days.

"Meet me for breakfast," she invited before sliding off the bed to stand.

"Depends. What's on the menu?"

"Croissants. Marmalade. Bacon and eggs. Jamaica Blue Mountain coffee."

"You splurged," he teased as his stomach growled.

"That's how I get you to come back."

"Works every time." He pulled her down to him and kissed her. "I'll shower and be there ready to chow down."

"You do that. And then afterward we can work off the calories." She winked and his desire peaked.

Dresden showered with Laxmi's perfumed shower gel. He'd forgotten his soap and would make do with hers. No one would know he smelled like roses and lavender.

Looking forward to a good meal, he hurriedly dressed. As he brushed his hair into place with brisk strokes, he heard singing. A woman's. Not Tonea's. He continued grooming as she played the song. The beautiful melody underscored the rich, soulful voice.

"Hey, Laxmi, turn that up. Sounds better than the original singer."

The volume rose a little and he settled back to his grooming while he enjoyed the rest of the song. Finally he came out of the bedroom to get a hot cup of coffee.

One song led into another. As he got closer to the kitchen, he had an aha moment.

"Laxmi?"

She stopped singing and smiled up at him.

"What a voice. You took over my soul in there. Singing with so much heart, so much sass. Damn, it was sexy."

"Thank you. I'd make a good karaoke singer." She handed him his coffee.

He shook his head. "I know an awesome singer when I hear one."

"Shush. Anyway, I was actually celebrating."

"What are we celebrating?" He noted her excitement that brimmed, ready to pour over into a pool of happiness.

"I got a call while you were dousing yourself in my soap." She sniffed his neck and giggled. "The manager for one of the hottest neo-soul singers is looking for an opening act. They saw Tonea on YouTube and followed up by going to one of the venues and liked what they saw. The spot is hers if she wants it."

"That's great news. I'd sing, if I could." He hugged her, tightly feeling his pride surge for what she had managed to accomplish.

"I left a message for Tonea. She's not answering. I think Phil is in town."

"Keep trying. She'll eventually check her messages. The important thing is she's gotten the breakthrough that many only dream of. I'm sure she'll call you back soon."

"A few weeks ago I'd be certain that she'd be happy about this event. Lately she hasn't sounded that confident."

"But you know she's nervous." Dresden did his best to sweep away her doubts.

"This is more than stage fright. It's as if she doesn't want to sing anymore."

"And you think it's because of Phil?"

She shrugged. "He's not helping her confusion. But she's not listening to me."

Dresden put down his coffee and held her. They stayed still in each other's arms. He wanted to fix all her problems and stamp out any distress that came her way. She worked hard and she impressed him with her stamina for the uphill climb to success. But he had to wonder after hearing her sing if she'd given up on her dream too soon.

He offered, "Have faith in Tonea. Remember she's stepping into adulthood with all the elements that come with that, whether she's ready or not."

"Yeah, you're right. Feels like decades since I was that young. Although it feels like the problems just multiply at her age." She eased out of his embrace and put a smile back on her face. "Let's eat."

Dresden didn't need a second invitation. He and Laxmi fed each other, giggling when food smeared each other's faces. He wiped the edge of her mouth.

In that instant he wanted to declare to her that he was falling in love. A big boulder dropped in his gut. One that was so unexpected it left him disoriented but also exhilarated. Although the revelation had hit, the emotion frayed at the edges with what it would mean for what was between them. Her reaction, if she was to ever find out, would probably not match his giddiness. He was sure she was too pragmatic about her life to accept his silly romantic declaration.

"What are you thinking?" Dresden probed.

She was happy over her deserved accomplishment.

And he knew she had achieved one of her goals. But now a quiet, reflective mood had descended on her. She was already working through the logistics.

"I just can't believe this happened. Sometimes, with everything that happened in my life, I think that I don't deserve success. Like I hadn't worked off my debt."

Dresden didn't interrupt. The bits and pieces that he knew of Laxmi's past surely guided her mind-set, guided her actions, maybe the fears that stood between them.

"Now that I got this nugget of hope, I don't want to let go. I'm afraid that it'll slip through my fingers before I even have a chance to enjoy it." She looked at him and then shifted her gaze down in her lap. "I've got to work harder. Put more time into this business. I can do this," she finished with emphasis.

"I know you can. You are determined. And I'm confident that this will not be your last success, no matter how much the doubts nibble away at your news."

She went on as if he hadn't spoken. "I can't afford to be distracted now."

Dresden knew he was included in all the things that could take her away from her dream. And he vowed he would not let her know the most important thing in his heart at the minute.

"I know it sounds selfish. I guess you have to be to get what you want in life. And so many times I have missed opportunities because I was otherwise focused." She stopped talking and sat up. "I can't relax until Tonea has given me the blessing to move on with this."

"Try calling her again."

Laxmi looked at him with a rueful smile. "In addition to the calls, I've been texting her. Still no response."

"Is it like her to be out of contact this long?"

"With Phil in the picture, nothing surprises me."

"Does she live far from here? Maybe we can walk." He looked out at the snowy cover. "Or we can ski over to her."

The worried frown evaporated as Laxmi laughed. "I sound like the pain-in-the-ass big sister."

"Not to me. Don't belittle what you do or have done for Tonea. You care a lot about the people in your life. It's beautiful."

No way would he say those three words that were secretly nestled in his heart. He would never play with her emotions or stand in the way of her dreams. His intention was sincere, but he didn't expect her to have the same feelings beyond general happiness. Breaking the terms and conditions to upgrade their relationship further wasn't in the plan.

Visiting, sipping coffee in the covered porch cocooned in a blanket of snow—that didn't rock the boat. Didn't create waves. Didn't make a fuss. He intended to keep it that way, as long as possible.

"You keep looking at me like that and I'm going to come over there and have my way with you," Laxmi threatened.

"Then let me try my come-hither look again." Dresden wiggled his eyebrows. He flipped back the large blanket that covered his lap. "Ready when you are."

Chapter 13

Dresden watched the colorful palette of lights play off the water. He'd seen Niagara Falls so many times that he no longer bothered to go to any of the public functions around the site. Taking the time to see it through the eyes of a visitor made a difference in his appreciation. Instead of him and Laxmi hanging out at his condo, he'd surprised her with the trip to see the Falls.

They sat perched on the sofa in a hotel suite over-looking the falls with an unobstructed view. The regular nightly fireworks display began with its illuminated pageantry over the turbulent water. Each cluster of fireworks exploded high over the spray with the tendrils of shimmering afterglow lighting the thick, continuous curtain of falling water.

"This view is fantastic and over the top. I hate to know what you spent." Laxmi cast a worried glance at him.

"Don't worry about it. I'll mow lawns in the summer."

"I'm a simple girl. We didn't need all of this."

"Would you relax if I told you that the Meadowses are paying for it? It's their suite and they are letting me use it." The admission still brought him discomfort, like he was a sellout.

"No way. Did I miss the memo of you making nice with the Meadowses?"

"Not really. Met with Grace the other day. Interesting. But it got me thinking about where to go from here." Dresden had spent time weighing what to do with Grace's generosity and the reason behind it.

"You mean like meeting with your mother?"

"No."

"Why not?" She pushed his arm. "Listen, you've obviously embraced Fiona and Grace."

"Overstating." Dresden's eyebrow rose as she stepped onto the minefield.

"Whatever. The next one is your… Verona. It's what you do next."

"I would have nothing to say." Meanwhile, his heart had created extra storage for all the feelings that popped up like annoying dandelion weeds.

"You're a professor. I don't think you'd be at a loss for words. Hell, I'll conduct the introduction." She picked up her phone. "As a matter of fact, why not today?"

"Don't you dare."

She punched in the code to unlock her phone.

"Do not cross the line," he warned. His frustration over the subject boiled over. Right now he felt the pressure building against what he wanted to do, with what he was willing to do. If no one stirred the pot to force a meet-up with Verona, he could exhale and ignore it. Maybe the sharp jabs to his conscience would cease.

"Excuse me? The line. I have a line?"

"I didn't mean it that way."

She looked away from him, staring at the falls. "I simply want to see you happy."

"Why do you think I'm not?"

"Because it bothers you to think about Verona. Whenever we talk about the Meadowses, you run in circles around not talking to her. As much as you say it's not a problem, it is."

"And you would know because... Oh, right, you're not talking to yours."

"Wow. You have no idea what's going on with my mother and me."

"Exactly. You don't say anything. I ask. You snap. I suggest. You snap. The only time that you don't snap is when I don't talk about the woman you won't speak to." He took a deep breath. "So until you have that fixed in your life, then stay—"

"Behind the line," she finished.

The passion over the topic deflated, leaving awkward silence between them. Somehow, during the discussion, their bodies had moved apart. Even the last fireworks display disappeared without any awed comments. The cold temperature outside had seeped into the room, frosting conditions between them.

Dresden wasn't waiting for her to say something. He was stunned with how far he'd gone in his anger and frustration over Verona. Where had that pent-up rant come from? And he'd lashed out at Laxmi as if she was the enemy. He wanted to get in his car and head for a desolate place to rage.

"That was not cool," he began softly. "I was unbelievably rude and unfair to you. I'm sorry." His voice grew stronger as he got through his apology.

"Accepted. And I must also apologize." She touched

his hand when he was on the verge of interrupting. "I guess we both have hot-button issues that aren't so hidden and out of sight as we may have thought."

"Yeah, I guess so." Despite the Band-Aid almost being ripped off, he didn't fancy having an in-depth conversation about Verona. And, frankly, he wasn't sure when he would have it.

That night they slept in the same bed, but facing away from each other. Dresden stared into the darkness, listening for the telltale puffs of her snores. Only silence hung over them with their breathing not in sync.

He was tired of being angry at Verona. It had affected him and played a part in his pushing away Laxmi. Sooner or later, he'd have to confront his inner demons. He hoped that it wouldn't occur after he ran off Laxmi with his bullheaded behavior.

Fix your own affairs before you fix mine.

Dresden's recent edict still echoed in Laxmi's head. The reverberations continued nonstop along with the weak timbre of her guilty conscience. Despite good intentions, she had opened herself up for criticism that she should have expected. It was easier criticizing and advising Dresden on what he should do. She could even feel proud of herself for encouraging him.

But to turn the light on herself, to fix herself, had her nerves on edge. The dread and reluctance slowed any feeling that resembled excitement.

All this talk about meeting with his mother, an epic reunion, repairing the damaged terrain between them, had backed him into a corner. He'd pushed back to get a bit of space. While, in her life, there was a chasm of undefinable depth between her and her mother.

Dresden had rightly accused her. She couldn't defend

her action. Since she'd left for Los Angeles, since she'd returned to Brooklyn, she had not sought out her mother. Though Laxmi had called a couple of times since her return to Brooklyn, she'd known there was zero chance of her mother picking up. But it eased her conscience to say she'd tried. The final parting when she'd left for Los Angeles had ripped her to bits.

Laxmi pretended that she'd healed. That her soul was intact again. And as time went on, she'd pushed the dark memories so far back that they were forgotten. But an intuitive Dresden had sliced through the veneer and let the harsh light show on her hypocrisy.

The revelation spurred her to action with this impulsive trip that no one knew she would take. Within days of her trip to Niagara Falls, she was off again. The plane landed at Dulles Airport in Northern Virginia. A short cab ride later, she pulled up in Reston in front of her mother's last known address. She debated telling the driver to wait. But she spotted her mother's Mercedes in the open garage.

She paid the driver and, with suitcase in hand, approached the front door. Unlike her house in Brooklyn with its solid brick exterior walls and heavy wooden front door, this house was made up of myriad windows. She could see into the living room and straight through its back windows that overlooked the man-made lake.

She pushed the doorbell, which sounded like a series of wind chimes. No one came into view. Laxmi leaned in and cupped her hands around her eyes to better see into the house. Nothing stirred; no one came into view. She stepped back and looked up, hoping but still dreading to see her mother peep from behind a curtain.

But no one came to the door. Not ready to give up, and since her cab was gone, she left her suitcase and trekked

around the side of the house to the backyard. A privacy
fence blocked the view and she opened the gate to gain
access.

She walked farther into the yard. Her heart pounded
as she entered the property. The lawn was immaculate.
Although winter had made its mark on the foliage, the
landscape was pristine with a professional touch.

Laxmi rounded the edge of the supporting beams holding up the deck. As she walked toward the steps, she
looked up at the deck and stumbled back in surprise. Her
mother, Carla, was silently following her progress from
her seat on the lounge chair. She had an open magazine
in her lap and a fruity drink in a tall glass within reach.

Laxmi waved and exhaled. She'd look foolish suddenly hightailing it out of there. As she got closer, she
could see that her mother was also shocked. *Good.*

Carla slowly removed her glasses. Then took a sip
of her fruity drink. Back in the day, there had been lots
of fruity drinks and lots of empty liquor bottles. Laxmi
wondered how much had changed.

Her mother looked the same, though her hair had been
changed from an orange-blond to a reddish-blond dye
job. The style hadn't changed from the helmet look with
a big curl that framed her head like protective gear. Age
was catching up, though, despite the nips and tucks. And
her makeup had a thicker look. But under all of it, her
mother always looked like a waif. Someone who needed
care and pampering, despite her normal childhood. But
she chose to hand over control of her life and choices to
her partners. Her mother never had a problem finding a
man willing to fit the bill.

Laxmi didn't rush to walk up the stairs. That would
require excitement and anticipation to see her. She had

gotten more than halfway up when her mother cleared her throat.

Carla said, "Please tell me this is a vision due to my lack of sleep and stress."

"Hello, Mother." Laxmi refused to buckle on the first slap-down.

"You're either a star and are here to rub my face in it or you are penniless and have come home to beg for a dollar." Carla always had a droll way with words.

"I hope you're in good health." Laxmi opened the door leading onto the deck. She closed it behind her and stayed in place. "May I sit?"

Her mother's shocked state didn't appear to show any signs of diminishing. She sized her up from head to toe, then toe to head, her thunderous scowl growing. "What do you want? You're upsetting a perfectly good morning."

"I came to see you." Laxmi edged closer to the other lounge chair that faced the lake.

"Why on earth would you do that?" Her mother wasn't kidding about the idea that it was ludicrous for her to come home.

"I wondered the same thing all the way here, from the plane to the taxicab. Why would I want to see my mother? Why take the chance when I haven't spoken to her in over four years? When all my calls go unanswered and no return calls are made by you?"

"I didn't miss you." Carla patted her hair, which hadn't moved at all.

"But I realized that what drove me here was to let you know that I've fallen in love. And for me to enjoy this magical feeling that I hope isn't a small moment in time, I must do my best to make amends."

"Love? You? Just because some wretched fool wants to rub himself against you, now you fancy yourself in love. Okay, that's lie number one. Next, you want to make amends." Her mother's throaty laugh was a familiar response that usually introduced a scathing tongue-lashing. Emotional abuse was her forte. "Maybe not a lie, but definitely a delusion, to think that you will ever be welcomed back into this house."

"No, not into this house. Into your heart. An acknowledgment that you have a daughter." Laxmi pressed her nails into the palm of her hand to stay levelheaded.

"And why on earth would I do that?" The often-repeated question wore on Laxmi's patience.

"It's a motherly thing to do."

Her mother's chin tucked in for the fight; her lips tightened into a flat line of displeasure. "Really didn't expect to see you."

Laxmi had gotten used to not crying. The skill came in handy, considering how frequently her mother wielded her sharp tongue. Along with holding back tears, she'd learned not to respond to full assaults.

"Have I ever been important to you?" The question popped out of Laxmi's mouth before she could suppress it like so many others she'd ever had.

Carla ignored her and gulped another mouthful of drink. Her hand shook slightly. "You shouldn't have popped in without calling first."

"Because you wouldn't have picked up the phone. If you did, you would have told me not to come. Was I adopted, left at your doorstep, sold to you?"

"You think you're Moses?" Her mother looked at her, squinting as if reading something on her forehead. "I carried you."

Laxmi waited for some sort of confession to fill in the gaps of her life with her mother. Her father had left the family before she'd gone to elementary school. Her mother's three marriages were a revolving door of men who were various stages of successful father figures but never a complete package. However, her mother's cold regard had been consistent for as long as she could remember, until Laxmi got the courage to pack her bags and head out to California.

At the time, she didn't think her upbringing was radically different. Her school friends and college friends had dysfunction in their lives, too, with parents, siblings or relatives. Some worse than others. But they'd all accepted it as part of their lives as they plotted their escapes once they were old enough and had the funds, or just armed with dreams, which cost nothing.

"Your father, my first husband, wasn't your dad. I was pregnant right out of college. He liked me enough to marry me and give you his name. It worked for a little while." She shrugged but her shoulders barely moved. "He left, and good riddance."

Laxmi eyed the fruity drink. She hoped that her mother no longer poured that poison down her throat, but if the drink had alcohol, she'd grab it and gulp it down to keep from swearing out loud. The desire to self-medicate through the revelation was strong.

"Finding a man with a young kid takes a lot of work. And I needed a man who could take care of me. You had your singing goals. I had mine, too. I was on my way to stardom with your father until I got pregnant."

"And you're satisfied now?" Laxmi didn't want to hear how much having a child had ruined her mother's life. Not again.

Carla shrugged; her mouth seemed to shrug, too. "I get what I need from Ken."

"Then you should be happy." Laxmi looked at her mother with a different perspective. The woman who'd barely hugged her, who hadn't offered compliments, who'd always celebrated her birthdays after the fact, who'd told her to get out and don't bother coming back for fear of running off Ken, had withered and turned into a fairy-tale witch. She wasn't pining for her long-lost daughter. She wasn't filled with regret. But she wasn't happy, either.

"Go. Continue living your life. You look well enough." Carla stayed quiet then said, "Love is overrated."

"Not if it's real." Laxmi found her voice and presented her defense.

"And you would know." Her mother snorted. "There you go with your uppity ideals. Stay grounded and you don't get mowed over by life."

Laxmi now understood that she had not been conceived in love. Hadn't been raised in love. And hadn't been cherished in love. Maybe it had affected the choices she'd made early in her career and when times got tough. But, little by little, she'd managed to crawl away from the self-destruction and find herself in the process.

She didn't have to fix this. But she did want to let her mother know that she was normal, loving and capable of being loved.

"Maybe one day, you'd like to meet my boyfriend," Laxmi offered as she stood.

"Expecting me to share cute stories about you as a baby?" Carla finished her drink and looked at the glass as if surprised.

"Yes. Somewhere in there you did find the ability to physically protect and care for me. You could have put me up for adoption and let another family love me."

Her mother looked down in her lap. "What's your man's name?"

"Dresden."

"Never heard of that before. Interesting to see what

kind of man has a name like that." Carla didn't look at her but gazed out at the frozen lake. Not much to see with the birds gone for the season.

"Okay. I'll leave now."

"If you got what you want from this visit, it's all worthwhile. I guess." Carla's voice trailed off.

"'Bye, Mother."

"What if I didn't give you what you came for?"

"Don't know. Hadn't thought beyond visiting you. But I wasn't ready to give up, either. This was important to me."

"You got spunk, kid."

"Would you like to have dinner with me this evening?"

"You're going to show off for me some more?" Carla asked, but there was a spark of interest behind her eyes.

Laxmi wasn't sure that she really wanted to have dinner with her mother. Maybe she was pushing things too far, too fast.

"I eat dinner at six o'clock. Any later and I'll get indigestion."

"No problem. I can send a car to get you."

"I may cancel."

Laxmi nodded. She didn't allow the disappointment to creep in. Her mother wasn't known for good follow-through with her commitments. But she would make the reservation for dinner and would sit and wait for her mother to show up.

Four hours later, Laxmi walked from the Marriott hotel at the Reston Town Center to the Mongolian Beef Restaurant. She waited for a half hour for her mother to show up. The taxicab had called her, as she'd requested, to inform her that no one had answered the door. She tucked away the heavy drop of sadness in her gut. Maybe a miracle could happen and her mother would still show up.

As the dinner hour descended and more patrons crowded the restaurant's lobby, Laxmi took the next available seat. She ordered her dinner and ate slowly. She just couldn't help holding out a smidgen of hope that her mother would turn up.

To delay going back to her hotel room, she ordered dessert. Sitting in the middle of the restaurant floor as a single diner drew attention. But when she was on the road with her career, she had spent many times eating alone in restaurants or in her hotel room. Sitting alone didn't bother her. She never craved being around people.

After dinner, she looked forward to the fried ice cream with honey drizzled over the crunchy coating. Laxmi breathed in the delicious sweetness and grabbed her spoon for a full dive-in.

"I wasn't hungry." Her mother stood at the edge of the table. "But I had this gift." She set down the box. "It's after six. Time for me to go home."

Laxmi threw caution to the wind, ignored her dessert, stood and hugged her mother for showing up. So many times, Carla had disappointed her, that she'd braced herself for one more time. "Thank you."

Her mother's body remained stiff for a while before her surrender happened and she hugged her daughter back. Then she roughly pushed her away. "I'm missing my TV show."

Laxmi nodded.

She blinked back the tears and settled in to enjoy her dessert as she watched her mother leave the restaurant. Slowly she pulled the gift close to her. She'd wait until she was back at the hotel before she opened it.

Thanks to Dresden, she had done what she'd needed to do. She had started the ball rolling to fix an important hole in her life. Her dessert tasted extra delicious. The mood in the restaurant was jolly. And Laxmi wanted to shout out her happiness and high-five everyone around her.

By the last spoonful, she decided to open the gift. Exchange of presents was a random occurrence, depending on her mother's sobriety. Carefully she pulled off the tape and then removed the gift-wrapping paper. In the box was a pair of pink crocheted baby booties. Under the booties was a photo of her mother holding Laxmi tightly against her body. Carla looked young and vulnerable, but fiercely protective of her little bundle.

Once upon a time, her mother had loved her unconditionally.

Laxmi fought the constant battle not to jump hip-deep into drama. But she obviously had a hard time listening to her own advice. Either that, or she was too stupidly in love to see nothing but the positive in what she wanted done.

She wished that she had the emotional and real-life support of Fiona. But her friend had canceled several lunch dates due to work conflicts and now Laxmi didn't bother rescheduling. Besides, she already knew that Fiona wouldn't approve of her current plan. And Laxmi didn't have the patience to wait for hell to freeze over before her friend accepted that she and Dresden were an item.

"Laxmi, is something the matter? Is it Fiona?"

"Oh, no, nothing. I just popped in to see you." Laxmi followed Verona into her office.

"I tried to get from my assistant what was the meeting for when you called. But she said you'd already hung up."

"It's about Dresden."

Verona's smile disappeared into a mask of stoicism.

"He doesn't know that I'm here."

"Maybe this is not a good idea, then," Verona suggested softly.

"No, it is. I want his happiness. And you control part of the reason that he has long-suffering sighs." Laxmi shrugged. "I'm sure that I contribute to his sighs. But I want to help where I can."

"And you think that I can help."

Laxmi nodded.

Chapter 14

FaceTime Thursdays were always something that Laxmi looked forward to because it meant sitting in bed, with the laptop in front of her, video-chatting with Dresden. Regardless of how late her day was, he'd want to hear from her. It was the perfect way to wind down for the night.

After a busy week so far, she looked forward to seeing his handsome face. They were in a good place, brushing aside their misgivings. She knew he wanted to see her more. And she wished that she didn't have to cancel on some of their trips. But he never pushed and she didn't have to feel guilty, although she did.

Dinner was light fare with a salad and a large fruit smoothie. She set up the video and dialed in.

Dresden's face popped onto the screen when they connected. "Hey, beautiful."

"Hey, handsome." She smiled at the sight of his mouth curving into that warm grin.

"How was your day?"

"Ah…hitting the road this weekend. This time we'll be in the city. A few hole-in-the-wall places may have a producer come through. Could be rumors. But I'm jumping on it before she has to go on tour next month."

"Good. Things have calmed down with Tonea and Phil?"

"Don't know. But I really find that guy annoying." Laxmi had grudgingly accepted that Tonea's groupie was now officially her boyfriend.

"He's just being territorial about his girl."

"There's no need. I'm not dating her. I'm her manager."

"Which is a 24/7 job."

"Well, that's the nature of the business. He can jump on or step off."

"Harsh."

"Why are you defending him?" She stabbed at her salad and stuffed her mouth.

"Be right back." Dresden moved out from the video and returned with a stack of papers. He looked up at her. "Not defending Phil at all. Don't even know him. But you've got to put yourself in his shoes. Remember what it's like to lose your good sense over someone?"

"Nope. No need to put myself in anyone's shoes. That's how you get caught up in not staying true to yourself."

"Not if you trust the person. And maybe Tonea trusts Phil."

"If she asked me, I'd tell her to push him back to the spectator lane."

"What if her heart asks for more?"

"Then you don't feed the beast." Laxmi laughed and sipped on her smoothie.

Dresden didn't smile. His attention was focused on grading papers.

"I'm going to get ready for bed." Laxmi barely held back a yawn.

"Good night, hon. Call me over the weekend and let me know how it's going."

"You're the best."

"Yep, I'm a good buddy." He disconnected before she responded.

She got up to take her dishes to the kitchen before she brushed her teeth.

Though she was stressed with work, it truly was good to have a guy who didn't push her. Dresden wasn't a good buddy; he was a great guy.

A man who held her heart if she had the courage to tell him. But she'd learned that offering up that level of commitment always came with consequences because you couldn't pull back, slow down, after declaring that side of things.

She'd have to love him as her own special secret that she couldn't share. Maybe one day. She hoped he didn't get impatient with where their relationship was headed. She didn't want to be one of those desperate women who announced their love in a final attempt to keep their man.

She shuddered at the visual.

Otherwise, it was another day of just talking to Dresden, secretly loving him and dreaming about the next time she would be in his arms.

Laxmi didn't suffer stomach upsets. All she wanted was for each facet of her life to flow smoothly. A day after speaking to Dresden on FaceTime, she had to deal with Tonea drama. She wasn't the type to chew antacids, but lately her run-ins with Tonea and her boyfriend had left her wanting to eat an entire bottle.

As usual for their recent meetings, Tonea was late. Laxmi checked her watch. She'd already texted Tonea that she was waiting for her in the car. The interview should have been over by now.

Finally, Tonea came out the building followed closely by Phil. He had his arm draped possessively around Tonea's shoulders. They took their time coming over to the car.

"We've got to get to the radio station." Laxmi motioned for her to get in the car.

"She's not going," Phil said with a smirk.

Laxmi pressed her mouth shut. She'd already made it clear to Tonea that she would not talk to Phil about her career. And changing direction on something they'd agreed upon was definitely no place for his input.

But her client refused to look her in the eye. Meanwhile, Phil hadn't diverted his gaze from her and his arm got tighter around Tonea's shoulders.

"Okay. So you're not going to the interview. Where are you going?"

"To be married." Tonea held up her finger where a sizable engagement ring took a prominent position.

"Married?" Laxmi turned off the car engine and got out of the car.

Phil dropped his arm from around Tonea and stepped toward Laxmi.

"I'm not sure what you think you're about to do. But I'd suggest for your sake that you back up. Today isn't the day to get on my bad side. And you are already crossing the line." Laxmi didn't raise her voice. Nothing in her demeanor suggested that this was more than a normal conversation.

Yet she fixed him in the crosshairs of her anger. The

arrogance he always had about him didn't fool her. She recognized a bully and a con man. But laying it all out to Tonea made no difference in the young woman's decision to keep Phil in her life.

The contract allowed for changes by either party under certain criteria. Replacing her with Phil was a stupid move, but she had stopped basing her business solely on Tonea's success instead of a more well-rounded set of goals centered around herself.

However, marrying Phil was an entirely different situation. An urgent one. Tonea's family didn't see Laxmi just as a business relationship, but one where their daughter would be cared for and protected from ass-hats like Phil.

"Maybe we should talk about this." Tonea, her arms tightly wrapped around herself, stepped into the tense space.

"You think?" Laxmi shook her head. "First, I need to call the station and tell them that you'll be late. Then we'll talk. You take care of business before doing dumb stuff."

"Yes, ma'am."

"Don't talk to her like she's a kid," Phil said.

Laxmi pinched the bridge of her nose. She prayed that she didn't let the full fury of her contempt rain on this man.

"Phil, can you take me to the interview?" Tonea raised her hand at Laxmi's immediate recoil. "Don't worry. We'll talk afterward. I'll meet you at the office."

Laxmi nodded and got in her car.

When Phil drove off with Tonea, she followed them all the way to the station. Until the contract was amended with Phil as manager, she would be and act on behalf of Tonea. When she got out of the car, their shock gave her the tiniest bit of satisfaction.

While the interview was under way, Laxmi sat in

a small conference room with Phil. The TV monitors showed Tonea.

"She looks good," Phil stated, but he wasn't looking at the monitor. Instead he focused on his hands, as his fingers feverishly picked at his sleeves.

Laxmi didn't say anything but returned her attention to the TV monitor. She listened to Tonea's interview. This time she paid attention to any clues she might have previously missed about Tonea's change of heart.

"You don't think I'm good for Tonea."

Laxmi still didn't say anything.

"I can settle on being Tonea's husband and let you remain her manager."

Why did he insist on talking? The more words that came out, the more she only wanted to punch him.

"My only wish is that she is not overused and pimped out to the highest bidder. And with all due respect, you seem to be replaying the steps that you made in your time. Tonea is a hip rising star. She deserves to be on the trendy shows, not this old-age stuff. Like she's already out of style."

Laxmi found it difficult to keep looking at the TV monitor. Thank goodness Tonea was almost done. Listening to Phil tried her patience. His observations had mirrored some reviews of Tonea's style and performance. Still, she refused to give him credit for any insight on her client's strengths or weaknesses.

"I'm not polished and sophisticated, but I don't have to be for Tonea's sake. And she's the one that counts. Marrying her is not about what you or her parents want." His tone hardened with emphasis.

Despite Phil's speech, Laxmi remained outwardly unmoved. Not until Tonea walked into the room did she rise from the chair. "So, are we ready to have a talk now?"

Phil sighed heavily.

They drove back to her office with her leading the way. She wasn't worried about losing her key client. Maybe it was Dresden's advice that kept her from falling apart over the possibility of Tonea leaving. Not that she wouldn't fight to keep Tonea, but she wasn't going to do so under these strange conditions.

And Phil qualified as a condition.

"Let's start talking," Phil said.

"No." Laxmi raised her hand. "I want to talk to Tonea privately. Then we shall take it from there." She pointed to the lobby. "You may have a seat."

She didn't wait for his response as she and Tonea entered through the private door to the conference room. She poured tea, fixed it to Tonea's wishes and then handed it to her.

"Thanks. You know me so well."

"It's my job to stay one step ahead. And, for the most part, I have done just that. But somewhere I slipped up with predicting this."

"You couldn't have known this would happen. I didn't even know that this would happen."

Laxmi gave a noncommittal shrug. A good manager would know. Should know.

"Guess I should start since…" Tonea sighed and settled into the chair. The hot tea was forgotten. "I don't want to lose you as a manager."

"And I don't want to lose you as a client. But we are at a place where we must discuss what it is that you want or feel that you weren't getting for Phil to imply that you're leaving. And it is always your prerogative. Yours." Laxmi wasn't sure where the conversation would go from there.

"Some days, I'm not sure I want it. I don't think that I want it bad enough to have the discipline to make it. Much less succeed. I feel…average."

"Average? But why?"

"It's some sort of feeling about whether I belong here. Whether I truly have the talent to be in the circle."

"I wouldn't manage you if you didn't. I'm teaching you the business as much as I can, and it is a business. Not just this life-defining moment. And my business, my company, is built to succeed. It's my livelihood. It's my legacy. It's my blood, sweat and tears. When I reach out and offer someone an opportunity, provide a partnership to reach his or her dream, I'm not seeking the average talent."

Tonea's emotions were not strange or unlikely. Feeling like a fake was normal. Even when awards and accolades became part of the experience, the feeling that she had faked her way or that someone would peel back the layers and see how deep the guise was always happened. And walking away was much better and safer than leaving herself open for discovery.

"Phil thinks that I should go into hip-hop. He knows a rapper who is looking for a girl to be on his mix tape. A featured artist."

"Some guy's shorty." Laxmi tried for a different tactic instead of full-on hostility toward Phil. "While it's great that Phil is thinking about your future, hearing about what Tonea thinks is what I want to hear. And always want to know."

"I know you don't like him," Tonea said in the singsong voice she used when she was about to plead for something to her advantage. "He's not a bad guy. Has a lot of passion. He's got his dreams and I've got mine." Tonea clapped her hands together. "Wouldn't it be wonderful if you repped us both."

"No." Laxmi cleared her throat and tried to soften the initial disgust. "Let's talk about Phil in a second. Right now, let's focus on you. I listened to your interview and you shared a lot more than you usually do. That's a good thing."

"I felt that people really don't know me. And I know we have the singing style of me being old school, like the next Sade and everything. I want people to understand where I'm coming from and what and who inspires me when I step up to that microphone. Otherwise I'm just another face." She grew quiet and still. Her gaze shifted to the now cold tea. "I don't want to be dismissed."

"Here's the thing. Some people will dismiss you, ignore you outright, may even disrespect you without cause. The nature of this business is to put everything that you hold dear on the line for the public to have their say with their support or not. That's the reality."

Tonea's shoulders hunched. A weighty sigh escaped in a quiet swoosh.

"Now, does the reality have to be the game changer for what you want to do in life? No. Not at all. It simply opens your eyes to the challenges. And you don't go blindly down your career path. But we all have fears. The important thing is not to be overwhelmed by them. Sometimes we can come up with healthy ways to mitigate the fears or we get therapeutic help to keep us focused. But the key is to move forward."

Tonea nodded slowly. Although she didn't say a word, she visibly relaxed.

"And with your feelings in such a turmoil, I will add

that maybe this isn't the time to be engaged to Phil. Besides, you have your first big tour, Miss Headliner."

"I'm petrified about that."

"You've got this," Laxmi reassured her.

"What about Phil? You should understand how tough it is to be with someone now. Weren't you in love with anyone while you were a singer?"

"Yes. I fell in love a couple times." Laxmi smiled. "I was too passionate about every guy for my own good."

"And…"

"I paid the price for falling for the wrong guy." She didn't want to go into details, but Tonea's possible walk down the same road pushed her to open up about her experience. "I put my life on hold to have a boyfriend. And when he felt ignored or not given enough attention, he pouted and argued until I felt compelled to change. The right guy will not force you to pick between your career and him. He will be confident enough to know that after the long day of labor you will be back in his arms."

"But he's so sweet and cares about every part of my business."

"And nothing's wrong with that. You're at the beginning of your career. You're planting the seeds for a bountiful harvest at some point. It's hard to balance both parts of your life."

"Marriage, kids and a wonderful home sound fabulous."

"And that's work, too."

"But you don't have any of that. I'm looking at everything that you gave up for your career, and now you're building your business, but still don't have anyone."

"I have Dresden." Laxmi cringed at her defensive tone.

"But based on what you said, he's not your priority. Not really. You are focused on the business."

Laxmi blinked at the blindside. With all her business insights and experience, she had managed to prove a point to Tonea that bit her back. How could she convince her that she could have it all when, as Tonea had said, she had nothing in her life to show she could have it all?

"Dresden understands my focus. And he's also not interested in anything emotionally heavy."

"You're wrong," Tonea stated with a matter-of-fact attitude.

"What?"

"He loves you."

Laxmi waved off Tonea's romantic notions.

"He told me."

"Now, how in the world did that conversation come up?" Laxmi refused to believe that Dresden would say those words *and* share them with Tonea.

"I asked him what his intentions were."

"You didn't."

Tonea nodded. "And he said that he thought that he loved you."

Thought.

"Then, when I saw him again, he said, 'I know it.'"

"He didn't say anything." Laxmi wasn't sure she would have wanted to hear that from Dresden. It was okay for her to commit to falling in love. She prided herself on being a survivor of broken hearts. To know that Dresden did love her, in return, thrilled her, but the idea that she was entering uncharted areas of her life scared her. She could love him. Was she worth loving, though?

"You know why he didn't. But you should also know that he does."

Laxmi hadn't ever had such a personal conversation with Tonea. And she still couldn't believe her client had talked about intimate matters with her boyfriend. Her boyfriend who loved her. She tried to restrain the smile that screamed from her heart.

Laxmi held up her hand. "Enough about me. Let's swing this back to you."

"I was only using you as an example."

"Duly noted. But let me give you another reason to put the brakes on Phil. Your parents will freak and then kill me."

Tonea looked shocked and then burst into a fit of giggles.

Laxmi had to laugh, too. That last resort was probably truer than anything else she'd used to get Tonea to change her mind about Phil.

"I won't let my parents kill you."

"Because you'd be dead first." Laxmi stopped laughing. "At least let them meet him, get to know him, before you spring the marriage thing. They've been pretty awesome with supporting your dream, investing in it and always being involved."

Tonea nodded. "I will."

"Look, we've been building momentum and I love that, but I think you also need to think over some things after the tour. Thankfully it's only twelve cities. So why don't you take a break after the tour wraps? You can then take Phil to meet with your parents and regroup."

"Will you let me go if I do take the time off?"

"No, I wouldn't let you go. Not at all." Laxmi reached over and squeezed her hand. "You're a special woman, Tonea. We're in this together, if you want it."

Tonea pushed back her chair and jumped up to hug Laxmi. "Thank you so much."

When Tonea had calmed and left, Laxmi sat in her conference room and stared out the window. Her main client had pushed the pause button.

Her business that had barely lifted off the ground felt like it was skidding along the tarmac with no braking in sight.

But Dresden loved her.

Chapter 15

Dresden opened the door to his office and looked at the genealogy chart he'd spent years working on but had put on hold ever since he'd received Grace's information. Asking him to continue his work was another ploy to pull him in, just like her announcement that he would be included in the will. Grace had more stamina than the average person. Refusing her felt pointless. And doing so on general principle made him petty.

Looking at the board, he charted where he would put the Meadows branch, with Henry and Grace as the anchor for that part of the tree, that part of his life. He stepped into the room and took a deep breath. Time to get back to work on his pet project.

A soft knock on the door and Laxmi's head popped in.

"Hey, babe." He offered his hand as an invitation to enter the room. They'd started alternating taking trips to visit each other. This time she arrived in Toronto for a quick getaway.

"So this is your secret project."

"Not secret. Just my personal thing." He still felt a bit uncomfortable sharing it. Each person revealed to be a relative came with the good or not-so-good details about his or her life. And in his parents'—Charlotte's and Patrick's—personal histories, the sordid characters certainly thrived and flourished. But as he dug into the Meadowses' past, he looked forward to learning how the families had come together. So far he knew absolutely nothing about his biological father. A mystery that he didn't care to solve. Maybe later. Maybe never. He barely could handle one parent's detachment. The will to fill the blank hole of his birth father's identity had dried up a long time ago.

"May I take a closer look?" Laxmi had already left his side and walked over to the chart. She exclaimed over details he didn't remember as noteworthy but for an unknown reason had caught her attention.

But now that she was there, Dresden was ready to close the door on his project. "Let's go out for dinner."

"You're such a spoilsport," Laxmi accused. "There's so much I want to ask about this. I'd wanted to do something like this when I was much younger." She shook her head. "Besides, I don't have the patience."

"Tracking family lines can be tedious and takes time. But really it's the history and the context in which they were born and lived that catches my attention."

"You should write a book about all of this."

"I do plan to."

"Even the Meadowses' side?" She grinned. "Wouldn't that be the tell-all exposé?"

"I'll leave that to the gossip magazines." Dresden had never been tempted to sell information to the highest bidder, although he'd been approached by many reporters after the birthday celebration.

"You have to take ownership of your family's story. Besides, I think that your historian credentials will add credibility."

"Thank you for trying to add to my workload." He walked up to her and pulled her into his arms. "But all I want to do right now is take you to dinner and then make love to you. I don't want all these people and their stories crowding into my precious time with you."

"Well, when you put it that way, I won't delay our departure another minute." She kissed him and skipped away as he held on to her.

Dresden didn't know why he had been tentative with Laxmi. They fit together so well that he couldn't imagine life without her. Yet she was in a neutral place, unaffected by him and whether or not he was in her life. Having her find him interesting wasn't exactly the same as someone who was madly in love, as he was with her.

"You're thinking too much." She smoothed his ruffled brow. "Let's go."

"Let's stay in."

"Nope." Laxmi smiled at his dismay. "You can't promise me food and then withhold."

"Cold pizza and sex, though?"

Laxmi snorted. "That's an old married couple's menu." Once she'd said it, she danced outside of his reach. "That wasn't a suggestion."

"Well, we're like an old dating couple."

"That suits me."

Dresden nodded, going along with her sentiment rather than agreeing with it. He would stick to their routine that guaranteed no surprise announcements to induce guilt or need for an even exchange.

* * *

Less than a week later, Dresden couldn't believe he was headed to another Meadows birthday party. No one, including him, would have predicted he'd attend his birth mother's birthday. But here he was entering the Meadows house where the celebration was already under way. Blame had landed at Laxmi's feet for her answering his challenge to reunite with her mother. She'd set the bar moving forward. In an impulsive attempt to impress his parents during their last phone call, he'd said that he was going, although he'd turned down the invitation.

"Good to see you." Henry greeted him with a hug and hard back slaps.

Dresden winced but nodded in return.

"Go in. Go in. The women are talking politics. Figured it was safer to man the door."

"Sounds like you may need a lieutenant." Dresden craned his neck to spy on the proceedings.

"Nope. It's a one-man job." Henry pushed him toward the living room.

He walked in and the room's conversation dipped as he drew most of the partygoers' attention. A smile couldn't form on his mouth. His face felt frozen; meanwhile, his heart pounded with his rising discomfort. Turning back wasn't an option. No matter what, he had to deal with his demons. Moving forward here meant he was ready to move on with Laxmi. A clean slate. So he went with a quick nod to various unknown faces.

"Good to see you," Verona said softly.

He offered her a nod, too. "I'm here."

"Would you like to meet my friends?" She was so tentative that he felt compelled to set her at ease.

"Yes." His smile naturally emerged to reassure her.

Dresden saw lots of faces, heard lots of names. But

he did his best to answer questions and offer his own commentary.

Fiona waved at him from across the room. The relief and happiness always seemed to be the reluctant partners whenever she showed up. He tapped his brow in a soft salute and her smile widened.

"You promised me that game of basketball. Then you were a ghost," Jesse, his cousin Belinda's boyfriend, joked as Belinda approached and slipped her arm around his waist.

"Enough already, you guys," she teased and greeted Dresden with a hug.

"Ready whenever you are, Jesse. Your soccer skills won't help you."

Invitations to join in social goings-on always felt like a duty before a sincere want to do anything. He didn't need to be handled by the group to feel like one of them. Not too long ago, he'd said he didn't want to be one of them.

Although he'd wavered over doing the right thing and the rawness of his hurt, he couldn't maintain the defense against the Meadowses' brand of family bonding. Who knew falling in love could liberate the soul? Every minute spent with Laxmi, every thought about their relationship, chipped away at his reasoning, his doubts, and excuses that he'd used as cement between the bricks for his wall. One good push and it would come tumbling down. He was ready to tell Laxmi everything that was bottled up in his heart. He took a deep, cleansing breath and focused on the party.

Standing in the living room with Verona only a few feet away and the thaw between them melting faster than he'd imagined, he could confess to being open to stepping into the group.

"How long are you in town?" Belinda asked.

"Here for two days." Dresden hadn't talked to Laxmi to find out if their plans had changed.

"Cool. We'll all play," Kent said, suddenly appearing.

"Who do you want on your team?" Dana asked. "And be very careful of your answer." She grinned as Dresden wiped faked sweat from his brow.

"Jesse." He didn't care about height or weight. He wanted someone used to hustling for the ball. Jesse's former professional soccer days would come in handy.

"All right. You're going for the scrappy type…" Kent said. "I've got you, Leo."

Fiona's boyfriend raised his glass.

"And what's the reward?" Dresden asked. Getting into the spirit of the competition, he quickly proposed, "We win, you will have a banging cookout—surf and turf." He thought the setting would provide a perfect launch for his entry into the guys' circle.

"Okay. If—when we win, you and Mr. Scrappy will go tuxedo shopping and shoe shopping for my wedding. It's a secret," Kent said after Dana meandered away to another group.

The collective groan spoke his pain. "Okay. Now, that's incentive enough for us to win." Dresden much preferred his prize.

"Don't hate. One by one, all of you will be tuxedo shopping." Kent pointed at each guy.

"On that note, where's the chips and dip?" Leo said as he wandered off in search of the snacks.

"Oh, sounds like the M-word is off-limits," Laxmi said, surprising him with her arrival.

"Hey, babe." He kissed her and pulled her closer to his side. "I got railroaded into a game of basketball."

"I've got faith in you."

"We've been working out," Kent said as he pointed back and forth between him and Leo.

"My man is ready and will whup your behinds." She looked up at him and in an exaggerated whisper said, "You are going to start working out, right?"

Their loud laughter drew attention. But Dresden didn't mind. The last remaining knot in his belly vanished as he joined in with the merriment.

"Can I borrow Laxmi for a minute?" Verona placed her hand lightly on Laxmi's hand.

Dresden motioned them on. He saw Verona also pull Fiona aside. Whatever tension had built up between the friends still hadn't dissipated. Maybe Verona was going to knock their stubborn heads together.

Personally, he was rooting for Verona on this matter. Laxmi had been stubbornly closemouthed about what had caused trouble between her and Fiona. Then he'd tried to get it out of Fiona and her irritation had seemed directed at him. He'd backed off.

He watched as they left the room. With no one he knew in the immediate area to talk to, he went into the dining room and fixed a plate from the buffet stations set up along the wall. On the hunt for a place to sit, he moved through the rooms and onto the patio.

Thankfully the mild late-winter weather allowed the option to sit outside for a few minutes before the cold seeped into a chilly experience. Anyway, he planned to devour his food in record speed. His stomach rumbled to concur with the probable outcome.

Deep into his third fried wing, he heard raised voices. Despite several people speaking over the other, he recognized Laxmi's voice. And he definitely picked up on Fiona's deeper voice. Then Verona's interruption sounded like she was trying to regain calm.

Dresden looked around for their location. All the windows were closed. And he couldn't see anyone in view. But a few people who'd had the same idea to step out onto the patio were also looking for the source.

Dresden set down his plate. Before the women said something embarrassing, he needed to warn them that they could be overheard. Although walking into an argument wasn't his ideal choice, he tucked away the dread and went in search of them.

Following the wraparound porch, he walked up on the three women heading back into a room. Good. Their discussion was over. They were going back indoors. He turned to go rescue his abandoned wings when Fiona said, "You're so busy thanking her for bringing you and Dresden together, did you bother to ask her how?"

"It doesn't matter. And I really hope that you're not acting this way out of some warped jealousy." Verona's voice was sharp.

"Jealous of what? You didn't want to meet him. You didn't want to talk to him. But suddenly you do."

"I'm happy he's here."

"Even if he was manipulated to be here. Tell her how you did it."

"Stop it." Laxmi sounded weary. More like defeated.

"She decided to multitask—get a boyfriend and fix his life."

"It's part of having someone in your life," Laxmi responded.

"Not when the only thing that attracts you to the person is how broken they are."

"How dare you accuse me of those things?"

"Does he know that you talked to Verona behind his back? Does he know that I told you not to mess with him after you slept with him after the birthday party?"

"Stop this right now," Verona said.

Dresden didn't believe in eavesdropping and stepped in before more revelations poured out onto the already sticky mess. A move, on his part, that wasn't about taking the high road. His anger burned too hot and intense. As his gaze looked over each actor in the drama, his emotion turned its focus inward on himself, spreading like a wildfire. Letting down his guard had its risks, but in his imagined scenarios of what could go wrong, he hadn't come up with this tragic betrayal.

"Oh, no." Laxmi looked at him, her hands pressed over her mouth, her eyes wide with dismay.

Even Fiona looked shocked before she hung her head.

Verona beckoned to him to fully enter the room that looked like a library and office. "Guess you've heard enough."

"I came to tell you that your guests can hear you." Dresden heard his monotone advisory. He heard it from a place where he'd retreated, as if in the last row in the nosebleed section of a stadium.

"We need to wrap this up, now." Verona took charge with a quiet will that had more force and results than Fiona's yelling.

"Dresden—" Laxmi started toward him.

"Don't." His hand signaled her to stay put. Somehow he managed to act sanely with a measure of dignity. Maybe a bit of Grace and her survival skills was active in his DNA. He continued, "I don't plan to stick around for the talk." Dresden wasn't in the mood to pick apart what exactly had happened and how he'd been brought into it. Those were the finer points to the larger issue: that he'd been betrayed by a trio of manipulators. But the crown belonged to Laxmi, to whom he'd given his heart.

"Don't leave. We were trying to make things better.

Please don't believe for one second that Laxmi did anything wrong." Verona held her hand out to him.

"Of course, you'd say that as the conductor of this sad duo." He turned to Fiona first. "Why? You felt it necessary to keep us apart because having Verona and me talking was more important?" He shook his head, terribly disappointed with her. They were supposed to be in this together, weathering the stormy conditions that they had no control over and dealing with what life handed them.

"It's not like that." Fiona gripped his forearm but he firmly disengaged her hand.

"And you…" He turned to Laxmi, unable to maintain a stiff, emotionally unaffected composure. The tears glistening in her eyes almost did him in. He shifted his gaze to her lips that she pressed together to stop their trembling. This wasn't about her. He was the target. He was the victim. "I'm not sure why I had to be kept in the dark about anything you did. If you thought I was going to get mad, then that's my prerogative. Maybe that should have been enough for you to stay out of this. But to hear that you did this to make Fiona feel comfortable and like you sounds like high school. This is my life that you all are tinkering with and pushing buttons as if I'm a robot. I told you once to fix yourself before you attempt to fix me. I was proud that you did. But you did it on your own terms, and without me instigating anything in the background. This is my life." He pointed at Verona. "Not hers." He returned his look of condemnation back toward Laxmi. "You had no right to do this." He shook his head, still feeling frustrated by the crashing, incoming tide of anger and betrayal. "You know what all of you need to get from this? I'm not into drama and family complications. I don't need this. Don't need Grace's money. Don't need someone who can't trust herself." He raised his hands in protest. "I'm out."

Dresden got as far as the porch toward the front of the house before he stopped. His body sagged against the wall as he fought to catch his breath. Running out of parties shouldn't be the norm. Yet here he was doing a sprint to put distance between him and the woman he loved.

"What the heck is happening in there?" Leo had almost run past him and he wouldn't have stopped him.

Dresden pushed away from the wall. He wasn't about to get into another conversation with someone about his life. "Let it go."

"I would if I could. But you're one of the family. And it sounds like Fiona has made a mess of stuff." Leo looked apologetic.

"You can stop with the cutesy sayings." Dresden also wasn't going to figure out the good guys from the not-so-good ones. His wounded heart wouldn't let him. He wanted to head back to Toronto and resume his boring life, to retreat with all his resurrected insecurities about Verona and the Meadowses, with all the tiny pieces of his heart ripped beyond repair over Laxmi, and with his faith in happy endings incinerated by this family.

"Fiona overstepped. She knows it, but pride has her putting her foot in it over and over again. But I think you probably took care of that with what you'd said." Leo continued to look apologetic and was doing his best to be diplomatic.

"You heard."

"The whole house heard."

Dresden winced. The whole point of him going to the room was to squash the argument. But he'd lost control and joined in the confusion. "I need to get my coat."

Henry stepped outside with his coat. "Meadows don't run, son."

"I'm not…" Dresden let it go out of respect for the patriarch.

"You're dealing with a lot. But you're not the only one. And from where I'm standing, each one of them is trying to do right by you. Some efforts might be clumsier than others, but there's no ill intent."

Dresden took his coat. "Thanks for everything." He hurried to his car before Henry dropped any more nuggets of wisdom.

He got in and sat for a moment. The message from Henry got through, but it didn't stop him from starting the car.

A loud rapping on the passenger window startled him. He looked over to see Laxmi motioning for him to unlock the door. He hesitated. Another conversation of explanation and apology wasn't what he wanted right now.

Space. Distance. Retreat.

She knocked on the window harder this time and he unlocked the door before his window caved in.

"Thanks. It was getting cold out there." She entered, rubbed her arms and turned on the heat.

"I can guarantee the temperature won't be any better in here." He rested his hand on the steering wheel and stared straight ahead. To look at her and allow for happier memories to intrude could threaten his resolve that this breakup was for the best. Painful, but necessary.

"What do you want to know? What do you want to hear? I'm here."

"Sounds like I heard everything about my life either from you or Fiona."

"I thought it was jealousy that had Fiona acting nutty. But I realized that she wants you to be part of her family so bad that she's become quite obsessed about it. And because I decided to do my own thing, thinking that I was helping her, she thought I'd screw it up. She had no idea that I'd talked to Verona."

Dresden couldn't deny that Fiona had come on strong in the very beginning until he'd pumped the brakes on when and how he'd be introduced by the family. It wasn't a stretch to think she had continued to be overly focused on him.

"But let's talk about you and me," Laxmi said softly.

"Let's not." He wasn't in the mood to do a postmortem on his feelings, much less with her. "This is beyond a token apology and 'let's move on' nonsense."

She continued, as if he hadn't protested, "My life has been a mix of potholes and sinkholes. Dodging either of those leaves me wondering if I've done so much wrong, then what have I done right?"

"Tonea."

"And she's signed with her boyfriend after getting the big recognition we worked so hard to receive."

"Ouch. But you can still have a business now that you've learned the ropes."

"Thanks to your advice. But when you came along, I felt like you were a shooting star. Enjoy quickly before it's gone."

"Okay, but didn't you see how orderly my life is? The time we spent together. The talks we've had. You have held back. I share what's in my heart. You take the information and then filter what you'll share with me. What kind of relationship is that?"

"One where I have a safety net in place."

He paused, surprised by the raw honesty.

"And don't you think you were doing the same with me?"

His head snapped in her direction. "A safety net with you?"

"You've emphasized how orderly your life is so much that I wondered why you wanted me in your life. But you expect me to change to make you comfortable. A slight adjustment here. A slight adjustment there. And I'm like Eliza Doolittle, being shaped into your desire."

"I don't want you to change." He had to confess. "I was being your alpha man. Letting the ego dictate the way to go. I thought I was doing a great job."

"Sometimes. But I like being in charge, too."

"And I have no problem with that."

"So what are we fighting about?" she asked.

"It's not a fight. A fight would mean there was something to win or lose. I'm walking away." He paused, but didn't surrender to being silent and wounded. "This is about honesty. And with honesty comes truth."

She averted her gaze, but then returned his with a determined hard stare. "Good intentions can be a worthy substitute. I don't know much about winning. Don't have much to show in that regard. But I am a survivor. And so are you. That's what we have in common."

Unlike the line of defense that he had when dealing with the Meadowses, his six-foot thick wall of obstruction, this wall between him and Laxmi was a loosely, hastily constructed structure. But he meant to create the emotional distance necessary for it to turn impenetrable.

Sitting near her didn't help with his goal. Despite the barren terrain between them, he was acutely aware of everything about her and all the subtleties that he'd come to love about her. He had to stay strong, shore up the defenses.

"Once upon a time, we had something in common. Or maybe that was the biggest illusion of this saga."

"No illusion. I didn't know that I could change. You know what I mean." Her words sounded like a plea. "We deserve our happiness. Pushing out the negative to get the positive…well, that's what we learned from each other. I'm sure of it."

Dresden felt a tug toward her. Her sincerity blew its magic toward him. He squeezed his eyes shut to block her influence. He struggled to reinsert Verona and his bitterness toward his adoption into the mix to maintain his anger. But the struggle was real. The struggle wasn't there. Only vapors remained where the obstacle had once been anchored.

Still, he treaded water, desperately looking for a safe shore where Laxmi couldn't reach him.

He pushed the button to unlock the doors.

She sighed and opened the door.

A loud rap on his window startled him. Henry glared down at him. Dresden had been so focused on Laxmi, he hadn't seen the old man approach with fire in his eyes.

Dresden lowered his car window.

"Laxmi, stay where you are."

"It's okay, Mr. Henry."

"Don't you get stubborn on me. I already have too many mule-headed grandchildren and their partners in this family. Looks like the eldest of the lot is the biggest one of them all."

Dresden swallowed his rebuttal.

"What are you bellyaching about? You've got a good woman next to you. Supporting you. Loving you. And you're sitting in your car like a pompous idiot, ready to throw it all away. And you know why?"

"No, sir." Dresden wished that Henry would lower his voice. The audience in front of the house slowly grew.

"You're scared. Don't bother blaming anyone for being

scared. Charlotte and Patrick, are you there?" Henry held up the phone. His parents glared at him through a video on the small screen.

"We're here, Henry."

Henry harrumphed some more, but didn't say anything else.

His parents didn't say anything.

The audience seemed to hold their collective breaths.

Dresden gulped. He might have felt a trickle of sweat going down his back.

Laxmi stirred, but also didn't say anything. But he did hear a giggle.

He gave her a side eye. Sure enough, her mouth quivered and another giggle burst through.

"This is not funny." He didn't know to whom he needed to direct his complaint.

"Does it look like we're laughing?" his mother said crisply. "Life isn't about achieving perfection. Never taught you that."

He recalled his mother's advice whenever things didn't go his way. Live with purpose, live with generosity, live with humility and live with love. His memorial wall of wounds and betrayal crumbled, a sad construction that didn't belong in the first place. He let it blow away.

"I think we've had a breakthrough," Henry told his parents. "Emergency averted." He ended the call, then looked at Dresden with a tender smile. "Now it's time for me to get back in there."

He fist-bumped with Dresden and left.

"Sounds like no one wants this ride to end," Laxmi said.

"And I almost did."

"You weren't getting rid of me that easily. I only pretended to leave." She leaned over and kissed his cheek.

"We're in this together." Dresden offered his hand as a gesture to seal their vows.

"Yes."

"No more secrets, especially when it deals with the Meadowses...my family," he said, and he swore he could feel his heart relax.

"Not even with the best of intentions, 'cause I understand what's important to you."

"And I'll be supportive of you and not play professor over your life and ambitions. I understand what's important to you," he declared without any regret or feeling that he'd compromised.

"Well, I owe a debt of gratitude for everyone who had my back. The Meadowses don't play when it comes to looking out for each other."

Laxmi nodded. "I love that about them."

"I love that about you, babe." He took her hand and kissed the inside of her wrist.

"Love you more," she replied.

"Think they'll miss us?" Dresden asked as he drove off, checking the rearview mirror for anyone waving them back.

"Nah. Grandpa Henry told them that Meadows men and women just like to blow off steam every now and again."

"It's all good, then," Dresden said, grateful for his tenacious girlfriend doing so much for his happiness.

"All good," she echoed.

* * * * *

KIMANI™
ROMANCE

COMING NEXT MONTH
Available September 26, 2017

#541 NEVER CHRISTMAS WITHOUT YOU
by Nana Malone and Reese Ryan

This collection features two sizzling holiday stories from fan-favorite authors. Unwrap the ultimate gift of romance as two couples explore the magic of true love at Christmas.

#542 TEMPTED AT TWILIGHT
Tropical Destiny • by Jamie Pope

Nothing fires up trauma surgeon Elias Bradley like the risk of thrilling adventure. But when he meets Dr. Cricket Warren, she awakens emotions that take him by surprise. And now she's having his baby… He's ready to step up, but can they turn a fantasy into a lifetime of romance?

#543 THE HEAT BETWEEN US
Southern Loving • by Cheris Hodges

Appointed to head Atlanta's first-ever jazz festival, marketing guru Michael "MJ" Jane sets out to create an annual event to rival New Orleans. Even if that means hiring her crush and former marine Jamal Carver to run security. Can love keep Jamal and MJ in harmony…forever?

#544 SIZZLING DESIRE
Love on Fire • by Kayla Perrin

Lorraine Mitchell cannot forget her heated encounter with firefighter Hunter Holland. Weeks later, she is stunned to discover that his father—a former patient of hers—has left her a large bequest! Despite mutual mistrust, reviving their spark might ignite a love that's as deep as it is scorching…

Get 2 Free Books,
Plus 2 Free Gifts—
just for trying the
Reader Service!

KIMANI™ ROMANCE

"You know why I'm here tonight," Lorraine said to Hunter
as they neared the bar. "What brings you here?"

"I'm new in town," Hunter explained.

"Aah. Are you new to California?" Lorraine asked. "Did
you move here from another state?"

"I did, yes. But I'm not new to Ocean City. I grew up
here, then moved to Reno when I hit eighteen. I lived and
worked there for sixteen years, and now I'm back. I'm a
firefighter."

That explained why he was in such good shape.
Firefighters were strong, their bodies immaculately honed
in order to be able to rescue people from burning buildings
and other disastrous situations. No wonder he had come to
her aid in such a chivalrous way.

She swayed a little—deliberately—so she could wrap her fingers tighter around his arm. Yes, she was shamelessly copping a feel. She barely even recognized herself.

"Oops," Hunter said, securing his hand on her back to make sure she was steady. "You okay?"

"I'm fine," Lorraine said. "You're so sweet." *And so hot.* So hot that she wanted to smooth her hands over his muscular pecs for a few glorious minutes.

She turned away from him and continued toward the bar. What was going on with her? It must be the alcohol making her react so strongly to this man.

Though the truth was, she didn't care what was bringing out this reaction in her. Because every time Hunter looked at her, she felt incredibly desirable—something she hadn't felt with Paul since the early days of their marriage. But unlike her ex-husband, Hunter's attraction for her was obvious in that dark, intense gaze. Every time their eyes connected, the chemistry sizzled.

Lorraine's heart was pounding with excitement, and it was a wonderful feeling after all the pain and heartache she'd gone through recently. It was nice to feel the pitter-patter of her pulse because of a guy who rated eleven out of ten on the sexy scale.

Lorraine veered to the left to sidestep a group of women. And all of a sudden, her heel twisted beneath her body. This time, she started to go down in earnest. Hunter quickly swooped his arms around her, and the next thing she knew, he was scooping her into his arms.

"Oh, my God," she uttered. "You're not carrying me—"

Don't miss SIZZLING DESIRE
by Kayla Perrin, available October 2017
wherever Harlequin® Kimani Romance™
books and ebooks are sold!

LOVE
Harlequin
romance?

Join our Harlequin community to share your thoughts and connect with other romance readers!

Be the first to find out about promotions, news, and exclusive content!

Sign up for the Harlequin e-newsletter and download a free book from any series at

www.TryHarlequin.com

CONNECT WITH US AT:

Harlequin.com/Community

 Facebook.com/HarlequinBooks

Twitter.com/HarlequinBooks

Instagram.com/HarlequinBooks

Pinterest.com/HarlequinBooks

ReaderService.com

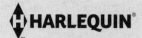

**ROMANCE WHEN
YOU NEED IT**

HSOCIAL2017